The Ghost Midwife

Murder at Rotten Row

ANNELISA CHRISTENSEN

The Ghost Midwife
Published 2018 by Dustie Books

ISBN: 978-1-9998173-5-0 (e)
ISBN: 978-1-9998173-6-7 (sc)

Cover and formatting for paperback by Timothy Savage
timsavagewrites.com

Reach author Annelisa Christensen online:
twitter.com/Alpha_Annelisa
www.scriptalchemy.com/
www.facebook.com/scriptalchemy
www.annelisachristensen.com

The Ghost Midwife

Murder at Rotten Row

(a novella of 20K words)

If you like this short story
and you like novels with strong female characters,
you'll love

The Popish Midwife

A tale of treason, prejudice and betrayal

a novel closely based on the true story of
Elizabeth Cellier during the Popish Plot, London.

Table of Contents

To Joseph, Carmen, Connor and Rhianna

While we try to teach our children all about life,
Our children teach us what life is all about.

~Angela Schwindt

Chapter One

Rotten Row

'Twas not I, the first to see her here in Rotten Row.
Nor was I the only one.

But I was the last.

For that reason 'tis vital you hear my account before measuring it against truth and all known things. On the Holy Book, I solemnly swear every word I speak is as it happened and, if I tell any lies, the Devil himself will come and take me. And I do not wish to meet with that one, though it was not so long ago I did think I had. For that reason, you can be sure I will not play false. Let your mind be open and hear this story to the end; only then shall you know all facts of the case. And, only with it laid bare before you, shall you add up all of the parts of it and see how strange it was for persons of our household, indeed for persons of Holborn and all of London city that came to see the gruesome sight revealed to us beneath our very noses.

I have warned you to be open, for I know you will doubt much of what I say, much as did my master and mistress, and all of the household at first, before we were convinced of the truth of it. Indeed, if I was the one to hear the stories and I had not lived through those times, I too might doubt them.

It did not begin with me but with another, the housekeeper, Mrs Thomas, who had the biggest fright in the whole of England. Even now, she can barely speak of the horror of it. I tell you, and I tell you true, the poor woman, who was never in her life prone to faint, was that day so afflicted we had to use the mistress's salt of hartshorn more than three times.

1

Yet, though it would seem the story started not so very long ago with Mrs Thomas, six months after Master and Mistress Appleton took up residence here, as I stand here on the brow of this day and look into the valley of the past, 'tis clear the true story had its source fifteen years since. 'Tis better, however, that I should reveal it as it opened up before us.

The following is a true and accurate account of the events as I know them.

Chapter Two

Mrs Thomas

The fire in Mrs Appleton's closet burned low. I dropped to my knees beside it, the material of my apron muffling the noise of the household items in my pocket as they clunked against the stone hearth. The arrogance of Jack, the master's man, that he should once again presume to order me to wait upon the mistress! I took the shovel from where it rested atop the Dutch andiron and, as a sword, thrust it hard beneath the fire-dogs until it thumped into the fire-back. I took little pleasure in the dull noise, preferring it to be harsher, so I loudly scraped back the heap of ashes and tipped them in the wood pail for Mrs Black's soap. Twice more I scraped clean beneath the fire, then added logs atop the dogs and watched them catch, all the while cursing Jack and his high-handed ways. At least I was given the task of stoking the fires today. The flames kept the cold from biting my feet and hands.

As I stood, I brushed ash from my skirt and apron onto the hearth, tutting at the streaks left there, and checked all other things were as they should be.

The candle in the wall-sconce was burned low and would need replacing before long.

Not waiting, I pulled from my pocket a yellow candle-stick and a blunt knife, dug out the old candle stub and dropped it in my pocket for Jack. If a person was clever, they could set one upon another and make a few pennies from them. Vexing as he was, Jack was a clever one. He was also an honest man and would give each of us a fair cut of his takings.

Before placing in the new candle, I held it to my nose and sniffed deep. The mistress could not abide the acrid smell of tallow smoke on her clothes and used only beeswax candles in her closet. Indeed, the honey vapor kept her dresses in fine shape and their sweet smell often gave me warning when she came quietly into a room, so I was confident in never being caught unaware pocketing candle stubs or any other such thing.

I took up the tongs and, with care, borrowed a small ember from the fire to light the new candle and dripped hot wax into the sconce. I then set the base of it into the hot liquid and held it fast until it was firm.

As I blew out the flame, such an odious screech — so shrill, so unworldly I dropped the tongs — had me searching every corner of the room for demons.

The clattering of iron on the wood floor made me jump again. The ember rolled free.

Shivering with fright and not wishing to be the cause of another great fire, I straight away fell to my knees to retrieve the tongs and throw the still burning wood onto the hearth, then rubbed the black scorch-mark with shaking fingers. The burn would have to be worked on.

Later.

Another scream, the same as the first.

My skin crawled all over. Blood pricked my face as it came out of it.

What was it?

After a short time when my legs would not work, I pushed to my feet and listened if there would be more. I never did hear such a noise, if it wasn't a dozen wild foxes in winter or a hog fighting its death on feast day.

Nay, not a creature. It was surely the scream of a woman so filled with terror I was loathe to leave the mistress's closet and discover what made her so.

Who was it?

'Twas not the mistress, for she was not yet returned from our good neighbour, Mrs Hunter, with whom she was wont to embroider and sew with ladies of high society. If not she, then it

4

must be one of Mrs Thomas, Mrs Black or Faith, for I was certain of it being the voice of a woman. But I could not move to the door to find out which, as I was sure I should. Upon my honour, I could not move until my legs worked again, and they were stubborn against doing so. Even though I took great pains to lift my feet and bid them take me where I wished to go, my shoes were as if nailed fast to the floor.

The two paces to the door were the hardest I ever took. Before I reached it, other footsteps, faster than mine, ran past. As I braved the passageway, the back of Jack disappeared down the stairs, leaping every other one. At last my feet were released. I followed, much relieved I would not be the first to find Mrs Thomas or Mrs Black murdered. If I must discover a body, I would lief I were in company, but still was I ready to flee should a murderous surprise meet us on the stairs with sword or knife.

Jack stopped. I stumbled as I tried not to collide into him, but knocked him forward so he had to catch himself. What he looked at I did not know.

The lights were low in the passage but they did not hide the eyes of the master's haughty forebears. Those men, his father's fathers, did never approve of me, no matter how exacting I was in my dusting and sweeping, and care not to lay dust upon them. It mattered not that they could not speak or move, for I thought them real enough, their eyes always upon me. Even now, I easily imagined it was one of them that had come alive from their oils and done some wickedness to the housekeeper or cook, such was the disquiet they gave me in that place.

With never a thought to his taking them, I touched my fingers to Jack's where his hand hung by his side. He did not take them, but still I took comfort from his closeness.

'Which way?'

It had not occurred to me Jack did not know which way we should go. He stilled himself to hear any noise that would give him a clue.

"Tis perhaps Mrs Thomas.' My whisper was not unlike a frog in the silence. 'She lay ready the table for the evening meal.'

'The dining room then.'

With that, Jack set off more certain, though it seemed he might be taking altogether too much pleasure in such horrors. Was he not concerned at what we should find?

'Hark! Do you hear what strange noise is that?' The words came as if they escaped my throat strangled with unseen hands. 'The like I cannot remember.'

Nor could I. It was neither a scream the like of the one we heard before, nor a cry, nor a snuffle, nor a sniffle. Nor even was it the moan of a person injured. The nearest I could liken it to was the whimper of a small infant child in the street that had too little in his belly to cry outright.

And it came quietly, over and over.

'You spoke true,' he said. 'It comes from the dining room. I should not wonder if Mrs Thomas does not lay injured and dying. If she is, you must fetch the surgeon at once while I tend her.'

I thought of the darkness outside. I had oft walked in the detestable dark, but not with the screams of a dying housekeeper chasing me through it. Though she was not yet murdered, picturing her so was enough to give me cause for fright, especially as I had never found myself of steady disposition. My heart jumped wildly and my legs still refused to move without uncertainty. Indeed, the very closeness to the dining room took my voice from me, so I could not speak. If Mrs Thomas did indeed lay dying, and it was incumbent upon me to run for the surgeon, rather I would find Mr Thomas and he should himself find relief for his wife.

Jack, that was always in charge of himself and others, did not feel it necessary to answer my whispered, 'I will go to the stable', or even nod, but took my wrist and led me to the open door, not letting me escape so easily.

Straightaway, we saw Mrs Thomas sitting on the floor with her legs sprawled before her. She leaned against the green, pine-panel wall opposite the window and nodded her head forward and back as if she were bobbing to the master over and over. I had seen hogs in crates that behaved that way. Back and forth, back and forth. That whimper we had followed to the room most assuredly came from her, though her mouth did not move and ran wet at the corners with white spittle. Her jaw was hard as if she grit her teeth. Jack strode straight to her, but I first peered into the dark corners of the room, to be sure nothing hid in the shadows. The tallow candles offered a lot of smoke but very little light, so I had to squint through it. Only once I was satisfied there was none that should not be there and, further, had bent low to peer beneath the table and made certain it was also safe, did I follow Jack to Mrs Thomas's side.

'Are you hurt, Mrs Thomas? What ails you?' Jack did not touch her, for her movement was strange and forbidding. She continued to rock and make that queer noise. She did not answer nor even seem to hear. 'Mary, kindly fetch Mr Thomas at once.'

Jack's voice was firm and urgent, heedless that, if he had allowed me, I would already have fetched Mrs Thomas's husband. However, if I did earlier take offense at his high-handedness, now his instructions were welcome, for it disturbed me to see Mrs Thomas in such a way and I could not move without being told what to do. At his 'Go on, Mary', I nodded at nobody and left Jack kneeling on the floor beside the poor demented woman.

I passed young Faith hurrying to the dining room and found my voice. I said to her, 'Best you get the mistress's salts, Faith. Mrs Thomas has taken quite a turn,' Then, without further ado, on I went to fetch Mr Thomas.

If I could have run faster through the house, without tripping or putting out the candle I took from the dining table, I would have done so. Mrs Thomas jangled my nerves and I did not like what I had seen. I would as lief not be on my own in the event that whatever had caused Mrs Thomas so much ordeal hid still in the shadows, or behind a half-closed door.

I crossed to the other side of the hallway to avoid each door.

When I came to the foot of the stairs, I forgot to shield the candle from the draught of the street door with my hand and it near blew out. The moment of darkness as the flame dipped caused such fright in me I took a breath and held it until it rose up again. I was more vigilant through the kitchen and out into the back yard, where the flame blew out but, with my night-eyes, I saw in the stables a lantern burning bright. It was great comfort to me someone would be there to greet me. Haste was of the utmost importance, so I trotted across the courtyard, slipping briefly in what was likely a horse dropping, and pulled hard on the stable door. It caught on a stone, so I shouted in.

'Mr Thomas, Mr Thomas, come quick!'

With good fortune, it was Mr Thomas, not Percy, undressing the horses after the master's long ride into the country, so I did not have to search further for him. Mr Thomas was a man I never did know if he was tall or short. Now, beside a horse of more than sixteen hands, he did appear shorter than other times.

'Bless you, Mary. What is it? What troubles you?'

'Tis not me, Mr Thomas, but your good wife. She is afflicted with some terrible thing.'

Mr Thomas stopped removing the blanket, faced me and frowned.

'Gads, girl! Speak plain. What is amiss?'

"Tis something horrid, Mr Thomas, but we know not the source of it. Mrs Thomas is possessed by some curse or misfortune and suffers terribly. You must come quick!'

Through habit, Mr Thomas placed a nearby bucket of water for the horse and threw the blanket onto its back. Then he stopped not a moment longer and was soon charging back the way I had come, with me fast on his winged heels holding the now blown out candle.

Upstairs, Mrs Thomas babbled in a tongue unknown to those of sound mind. Her strange voice came to us even as we ran along the corridor. Momentarily, as we arrived at the door, she stopped and groaned.

When we entered the dining room, Jack was withdrawing the salts from beneath her nose. He came to his feet and stood back next to Faith so Mr Thomas could set himself down beside his wife. Faith was so very still, one arm across herself and clasping the arm that hung by her side. Gently, and without comfort for her alone, I took her loose hand and she, without looking from Mrs Thomas, turned it and clasped mine.

At the same time, the stableman took his wife's hand. She did not at first answer him, but continued that strange bobbing with her head. Then Mr Thomas took her face firmly and made her look at him. He spoke low and quiet, so we could not hear the words, but I determined they were words of comfort oft spoken between a man and his wife.

After some little time of this, with Mr Thomas voicing such gentle kindness and sweet compassion in his wife's ears, her eyes came from far away and she looked at her husband.

She screamed so loud, and so sudden, her husband fell back over his heels onto his backside.

My heart drummed so that, for a while, I could not hear a thing that was said. I did not know if to run from the room or further into it. I looked over my shoulder. If she had screamed at something she saw there, I should run. I would run from this room to the bedchamber I shared with Faith and lock the door. But what if the horror stood right behind me, between me and the door? If that was so, I should move closer to the others for safety.

Search as I might, nothing but unease and imagined things moved in the shadows.

Having released the scream as if it had been trapped inside her, its echo coming back to us from the walls, Mrs Thomas covered her ears. She spoke to Mr Thomas.

"'Twas a... a terrible abomination,' she said. ''Twas the Devil come for me.'

'Was it perhaps a thief, my dear? Was it a burglar?'

'No! No. If I tell you it was the Devil, then that is what it was! There it was, plain as you are now. It... it...'

And then she fell to gibbering once more, until Mr Thomas could again find her in her head and bring her back.

"Here,' said Jack, 'what's happening to her now? Why does she shake so much?'

'Perhaps she is bewitched,' I said.

'Tell me plain, woman, what has addled you this way?' Gentle and steady, her husband once again held the sides of her face in both hands.

'Likely 'tis the fright of it, whatever 'it' might be!' Jack confided, saying what was plain to see. I moved slightly forward so I could see his face and was not surprised to see his nerves were not at all stretched. That did not last for long.

Alarming us all, Mrs Thomas started waving her arms and hands straight out before her as if she ran blindly through the thick undergrowth of a forest at night. It was as if she protected her face from branches, spider webs and other things unknown, unseen. In a room with naught but a few folk concerned after her health, it was a very peculiar sight.

Then she put one hand behind her on the floor and, with her back still against the wall, pushed herself to standing. Mr Thomas fast stood up beside her and before she took flight grabbed hold of her and held her close. For the slightest of times she stood rigid, then she went limp in his arms and cried, and in the crying repeated her words about the Devil coming for her soul, and how she had never done a thing in her life to deserve his taking such an interest in her. The way Mr Thomas held her was as if she were a new-born babe. It made him seem taller.

Jack frowned, as did I. Faith, still holding my hand, moved behind Jack, so I was standing next to him. I could clearly see how he puzzled over the events of the night and tried to fathom the housekeeper's nonsense.

When Mrs Thomas stopped her sobbing, and she and Mr Thomas stood quiet and still and locked together as one, I thought to steal myself away and leave the man and his wife on their own, but some part of me desired the whole of the story from beginning to end and I could not make myself go. As well, I did not wish to go into the corridor alone. I stopped myself hopping from foot to foot, not knowing what I should do, and looked to Jack to see if he too waited or if he would signal we should go. He did neither. When he saw my raised brows, he pointed to the far side of the room beyond the dining table and bobbed his head for me to follow, which I did, pulling Faith along behind me. It was proper to put some distance between ourselves and the two clammed tight in each other's arms and, for a short time, I was less uncertain of it all. Until Jack next spoke, that is.

'If this be where the apparition stood,' he said, ''twas naught but light and shadow.' Jack pointed at the shadows cast by the fire I had stoked up and set a-crackling an hour or more since. 'Look here,' he said louder for the benefit of every person. 'This is what you have seen and what has had you in such convulsions!'

The log before the fire threw shadows into the room that were huge then small then huge each time a flame had occasion to lick the side of the log behind it. Indeed, with no proof of any demon, it did appear Mrs Thomas must have imagined what she had told to us. Or perhaps her eyes did not serve her so well as once they did.

Mr Thomas looked first, then he whispered to Mrs Thomas to look. I found myself glad to have good reason for Mrs Thomas's fright. That was until Mrs Thomas croaked, ''Tis not the creature I saw. I tell you it was the Devil himself.' She stuck her face back to her husband's shoulder and did not look up again. His hand went to her head and he stroked her down like one of his horses, then he rested his chin on her head and held her close.

I too doubted that a shadow we knew every day could be mistaken for the Devil.

Whether it was the Devil, or if it was not, though Mrs Thomas was the first to see such sight, she was not the last.

Chapter Three

Faith

A week after the incident of Mrs Thomas's visitation, Faith ran squealing and squawking through the house.

'It comes! It comes!'

Never before was there such commotion. Every lady, gentleman, servant and guest came fast to Faith's rescue. Bless my soul, if she wasn't a sight.

After Mrs Thomas was in the throes of terror, when she was discomposed as before-mentioned, no servant bore well being alone in the house by candlelight. If we were able, we worked in pairs. The winter nights stretched a very long time, too long. But most passed uneventfully in slumber if our work was done and the mistress generous to let us go. The worst time was between the setting of the sun and the time when sleep took me from my busy thoughts until morning light.

On this occasion the house was neither dark nor frightening in the normal way of things. Flickering shadows from the fire were dulled by grey forenoon light through the windows. So, none was prepared to be fearful of another incident such as was had by Mrs Thomas.

Merely that I was in a room nearby, I came upon the poor girl first. I am bound to say she was afflicted in the very worst manner.

Some of Faith's hair, no longer held with pins, fell to her shoulders, while other of it stood in the air like uncarded wool. But it was Faith's countenance that took me aback. Apart from Mrs Thomas, I never did see such fright, such terror, in a person's eyes. They stood so wide, and rolled back so far, they showed two rising, white half-moons. Her skin had little more colour than her eyes. If

I was not so familiar with the face of my fellow maid, I might have thought she was herself a ghost come to haunt us; and a banshee would make less noise! I was obliged to cover my ears every time her scream made them buzz like a bee so that, when I shouted to her, my voice came back at me inside my head.

'Faith! Faith! Why do you—?'

With a start, she made as if to run past, so I dropped my hands from my ears and took hold of her arms to shake her, but was myself shaken by a scream louder than all before. Her horrid eyes saw not me but something beyond me. I fast turned my head in the case some creature prepared to leap upon me. Nothing. Neither did she run from any terrible or frightening thing behind her. If what had frightened her lurked here still, then it was not in plain sight. That did little to remove the fear she imparted to me, and my first thought was to stand closer to her. Instead, I shook her harder.

'Faith, I am here. I am here. 'Tis only you and I, none other. Tell me, what has caused you this unparalleled distress?'

Even while I held her arms, she lifted her hands and covered her face, sobbing loud enough to scare away every scavenging rat throughout Rotten Row. Still she answered me nothing I could understand.

Such madness, twice in too few days.

I was never so glad, then, to see first Mr Thomas and Jack, then the master and mistress of the house accompanied by Mr and Mrs Stonely, the guests treating with them. Soon after came Mrs Black who, interrupted in preparing her daily batch of cheat bread, cupped together hands hanging with misshapen lumps of dough she had been kneading. Percy, the stable boy, came behind her, moulting straw upon the recent-scrubbed floor boards like a scrawny, mangy dog in the summer. Mrs Thomas did not come. Jack later told me she did not wish to ever again set eyes on that one she saw a sennight since.

All of these people stood around Faith and myself and, even though she had stopped screaming, Percy made a play to Jack of covering his ears and pulling a long face. Jack grinned at the lad then turned back to us and watched what would unfold. He told me some days past he did not for one moment think what Mrs Thomas saw could be anything unnatural and was adamant we women were as skittish as horses worried by a snake.

For some little time, I did find myself with so many eyes upon me, expecting me to make whatever effort was necessary to calm or quieten the girl. With awkwardness I was unused to, I patted her back, smelling the hot odour of sweat mixed with the lye soap and starch of her clean clothes. Still she heaved but, as if she were a child, she turned and dropped her forehead to my shoulder. She took me tight around the waist in her arms and wept relentlessly so that I wondered if we should all drown in her tears. I was grateful when Mrs Black broke from the circle around us and fetched a stool for Faith and sat her upon it. Mrs Black was more natural a mother than I, so I shuffled behind her and let her mollify the poor stricken girl with some soft words, a handkerchief from her pocket and a pat on her shoulder.

Faith's tears stuck the dress fabric to my skin, and I wiped my shoulder with the duster in my pocket. Like a witch's spell, Mrs Black cast a blanket of comfort over the girl in the way only a mother of many children could. We all of us moved closer when Faith started talking; only our utter stillness, quieter than a cat hunting a mouse, allowed us to hear her shaking whisper.

'Twas Mrs Thomas's Devil, though it was not Mrs Thomas it wanted, but Mary. I tell you plain, it came for Mary.' Faith turned until she had me full in sight. With the calm face of an ancient sage, and not her face at all, she lifted her hand and pointed at me. 'It comes for you, Mary. You should leave here. It comes for you.'

Her conviction cast part of me in ice, part of me in fire, and where the two met I melted inside.

When Mrs Black took her face and turned it toward her, the girl became young again, a child answering to an adult, with hardly a breath in between. 'I swear, Ma'am, there was no thing or person in the corridor when I came here, and none could be here without me seeing it, for I faced both doors from the far end as I dusted the paintings. Mrs Thomas told me... she said I must mind the corners and not miss them as some are wont to do.' With that last, I swear her eyes accused me. I searched for words to defend myself and tried not to stick out my tongue at her, but she went on. 'And that's what I did, what I was doing, but though I worked them with my full attention, I am certain, with certainty most clear, I would have known if any had entered while I worked. I would have seen something, felt something. You know when a door is opened, don't you? How it sends a draught over you?'

'Yes, girl, we know that. Go on with your story. What happened?' Mrs Black patted her hand.

Faith's bottom lip quivered, and I was afeared she may cry again, and we might never know the full events of the morning! She wiped her long nose on the back of her hand and I tried not to see it shining. I thought of my wet shoulder. She looked up at Mrs Black and, as she had done before, the cook patted her hand... where it glistened with wetness. When she did not wipe it, I could not prevent myself from wiping down my own hand on my dress. It did not help. Faith sniffed hard and went on with her tale.

As if for a recital she said all in one piece and we listened in silence.

'It was when I reached the painting opposite the door, I had this... it was like... it was a knowing, like when the mistress, beg your pardon ma'am,' Faith nodded to the mistress, 'happens upon you when your task prevents her going to where she would go, but you cannot let her past, for she would slip on the wet floor you are washing, so she must wait for you to complete your task. And you know she's there watching you and waiting for you to do what you must, even if you have not once taken your eye from the floor. It was like that. I knew someone was watching me, and I thought it was the mistress or master, for they did not speak to me, but then the hairs on my arms and my neck prickled and the air became so cold I shivered, for I remembered the master and mistress were entertaining in the parlour and, in any case, could not have passed me to that end of the passage.'

Mrs Black shifted so I could not see Faith. The master and mistress were discomforted and looked to the end of the corridor as I had done before and found myself compelled to do again. The unknown presence was almost palpable. But the corridor was as it always was in the morning, with daylight from the door-light behind us reaching out toward the wall at the end and falling short, and there was nothing of any importance in that place. While I was far from disappointed that no unnatural being graced us with its presence, I also found I was somewhat unsatisfied by the further lack of any proof of it.

With Mrs Black's prompting, poor Faith gave an honest account of herself and what she saw, and none had any doubt but that she saw something that put her in such a sorry way. Indeed, if that creature that watched her were to show itself when we all stood so strong together, we might not have been afraid of it at all. But, alone, not one of us there would be any more brave. In any case, that was not its way, as we were to discover.

None ever saw it in company. And what each saw was not a match for that of any other. Faith's ghost, for it could be described as none other when it appeared with no sound nor warning and was called from this world as quiet as it entered, said nothing but made a sound the like of my name. Though Faith swore it must surely be Mrs Thomas's Devil, it cast not the same shadow nor did it move in the same way. Instead, it watched her and, when she looked up, she saw it had eyes. I could not remember if Mrs Thomas said her ghost had eyes, and I did not ask her about it, for she would tremble each time any dared speak of it in her presence, and she would be cross and shout oaths at everyone around her, swearing we had fun at her expense and we should stop it with immediate effect! However, later I discovered something more about it.

'What was it, Faith?'

That night, as I brushed my hair without a mirror, for Mrs Thomas had ordered every mirror covered with a sheet in order to discourage the spirit from dwelling there, I examined the younger maid. She had only lately come to Rotten Row from Cheapside, and now lay tight-wrapped as a swaddled babe in her blanket. Only the white skin around her eyes shone in my candle's light, still waiting for the blood to come back into it. Faith's haunted eyes watched me. She did not answer. She had avoided me this afternoon, for what reason I could not fathom. And on one occasion when I had spoken to her she had moved toward Mrs Black and did not answer. But she could not long avoid me tight together in our room.

With my own eyes, I measured the distance to my bed, lifted my night-dress and hopped bare-footed over the floor onto the mattress. The empty darkness beneath the bed had me imagining all kinds of things that might hide there or appear from nowhere. I would not stand close enough to give anything beneath the bed a single chance to reach out and grab my ankle, to perhaps drag me down into Hell's roasting fires.

'I mean, what you spoke of before...' This came in heaving breaths after my exertion. 'Was it evil, as Mrs Thomas said?' I immediately wrapped the blankets around me, the cold and damp in them making me shiver. She answered at last.

'Yes, of course. But do not have me dwell on such wickedness, Mary, for I shall have trouble enough closing my eyes even now, without further thought upon it. 'Tis certain I shall not sleep any time this sennight.'

Such answer did not satisfy my curiosity. If the house was haunted, I must know all I could about the creature that preyed upon us. And if the spirit had come to dwell there, I was certain as Faith I would sleep neither tonight nor any night until I left there.

'Nor I, Faith. And for that very reason, I would know more about it not less.'

'You ask altogether too many questions. All I know is what I have told you.' After some silence she added one thing more. "Tis my belief 'tis a murdered soul searching for the one that took its life.'

With curiosity, I heaved myself up and leaned on my arm. 'Whatever gives you such a notion?'

She did not answer directly, but I then discovered why she had avoided me. 'Did you murder someone, Mary?'

'Not I,' I said. Whatever made her say such a thing! 'Are you mad? I never had reason to murder any person in my life. 'Tis a sin

17

of the worst kind. Why do you accuse me? I forgive you only that you are not yourself, but I will not have you cast such aspersions on my good character.'

'Forgive me?' she said. 'It called your name. Why else would it be seeking you?' Her voice was high. 'I have heard a murdered soul will come back and haunt its murderer.'

I lay back down and pulled the covers tight round me, tucking them securely beneath my back then, pulling it over the top of me, clasped the other edge close to my chest. 'If murder was done to a person, I had no hand in it.' My voice was muffled even to my own ears. 'You are quite mad, Faith. 'Tis the fright speaking. We will speak of this another time after all. Go to sleep.'

Then it was the turn of Mr Thomas to witness the unnatural, which seemed to find him in a way he rather it had not.

'I will not test your faith in what I am to tell you, for I did doubt my own eyes in this, although I have the most reason not to. If I ask you to bear with me, 'tis only for reason I am unaccustomed to hear myself speaking such nonsense. Even the great Mister Shakespeare himself, with all his fairies and ghosts, would look at me askance if I told to him with such earnestness what I have witnessed.'

Mr Thomas stood beside us while we ate, but eating had become of secondary importance in the face of a story that had some of us swallowing our last bite with difficulty. Not Jack, though. His hunger would never be left unsatisfied for a ghost story.

'Mr Thomas, tell us do. We are all agog to hear it. Is it quicksand you skirt with such nimble feet? Nay, 'tis a story that affects every one of us.' Mrs Black came back to the table with another loaf of household bread, placed it on the table with a clunk in front of us, balled her fists and dug them into her waist. 'And if you delay the telling of it, you can be sure your dinner will be delayed another minute for every minute you would have us wait.'

The stableman did not wear his periwig, but held it loose in his hand like a duster. His usual commanding nature had gone away and in its stead stood a disturbed and distracted man, the short Mr Thomas, his thin hair in equal disorder.

'Aye, Mr Thomas, tell—'

I was cut short by Jack.

'Shhhh…' Jack held up his pointing finger. 'Shhhhh… Hark. Do you hear?'

Between the breathing of the house, those common noises we were used to hear every day, there was… nothing.

'Do not tell me—' I said.

'Shhhh…' he said again, this time waving his hand fast up and down to show his urgency.

I shushed.

We all did.

We stilled so I could not hear even a breath.

Into the silence came a noise I did not know. Not footfall on the floor boards. No. Irregular and disturbing, this tapping did not belong. I looked to the kitchen window but, and I knew it before I cast my eyes there, no tree lay close enough to tap on the pane. I turned my head slowly to discover what it was that made that noise. As I turned, the stillness of the group, unnatural as the sound, gave me to take a slow breath. Fear crawled up my legs and back, along arms and scalp, pricking the hairs as they stood on end.

I shivered.

Someone gulped. It was not me, but made me think of it. I closed my own mouth and swallowed. It was troublesome, my mouth being so dry.

'What is it?' Mrs Black's whisper was so loud I wanted to hush her, but could not make a noise. The tapping stopped. Some minutes passed and no more noise came, then Jack let out his breath, shaking and sharp. Straight away, every other one of us let out the air we held, then drew it right back and held it in again in order to keep our vigilance.

'What is it?' Mrs Black whispered again, barely heard. She growled in her throat then said it a third time a little less hoarse. 'What is it?'

Mr Thomas answered. He could do no other when every eye was upon him. "Tis 'it", he said. "Tis what you think it is.'

He rubbed his forehead, then ran his hand back forgetting he held his periwig and, as if it surprised him, dropped it to the floor. He picked it up. What he would have said was stopped in his mouth when he raised himself up again and saw Mrs Thomas. He did not take his eye from her as he spoke.

'Mrs Thomas and I will be leaving.'

Mrs Thomas, who I had not thought to cast an eye over before now was as a stone statue. Her face twisted as a gargoyle.

I still could not swallow.

'Leaving? Now? You cannot.' said Jack.

'You think it was that—?' I said.

Mr Thomas chose to answer me.

'Aye, I do. It was.' Mr Thomas moved around the table to his wife and cupped his hands over her shoulders. 'Some perverse thing has come to this house. If it means us harm or if it does not, I cannot tell, but I will not have us live longer in this unnatural place.'

'What was it you saw?' Jack placed his hands on the table and leaned heavily upon it, his head level with Mrs Thomas, but facing up to her husband.

'What I saw was not born of this world. Whence it hailed from I know not.' He breathed hard. "Twas a light that hung as high as a lantern held by a man, but as God is my witness, none held it.' Mr Thomas stopped talking and in the silence came the echo of that tapping, though I did not hear it with my ears, it beat in time with my heart. 'It flew one way, there.' He pointed at the wall away from the door. 'Then t'other way, there.' Mr Thomas marked the path of it across the kitchen with his hand. 'A circle of burning light, flying as a bird flies from wall to wall. Then it was up there in the beams, a sun so bright I was obliged to shield my eyes from it. It made no noise and said nothing.'

I looked up at the beams expecting some mark of it to remain, perhaps a scald or a trail, but there was no sign of it. That did not stop the others looking where he last pointed too.

'A burning fire, as in the Bible?'

Jack turned to see who spoke, for Faith's voice was not her own. She was uncommonly calm, as she had been when she had seen her ghost. If I had not seen her so completely undone, I would have thought her the bravest amongst us. As well, I had shared a bedchamber with her every night since, and knew her to be afraid of every noise and creak of floorboard. Her stillness was the same as that of Mrs Thomas. It came from fear so deep it was beyond the understanding of those that had not witnessed the same.

Mr Thomas answered Jack. 'It did not speak to me in the voice of Our Lord. It did not speak to me at all, I tell you. Though I spake to it, and asked it, 'What will you have of me?' it stayed silent.' He too became silent. Then he repeated his earlier intention. 'Odds teeth! We cannot, will not, stay here longer. I will see Master Appleton on the morrow and give our notice.'

When only Mrs Thomas and Faith stood witness to that dark spirit, none other in the house inclined themselves to be rid of it. But when next Mr Thomas, and later Jack, became its targets, and Mr Thomas's hair stood on end and Jack's hair turn white, we servants agreed with Mr Thomas, we should do better to find work in a house where no horrid other-world spirit haunted us. Thus, with the consent of all staff, Mr Thomas went and informed the master of our agreement in this. The master, 'not owning to such nonsense', raised the wages of all the staff then held a discourse with the mistress and lent the reins of it to her. She, in turn, sent a runner to knock on the door of first one then another of our neighbours to beseech each to come to our aid.

Our plight preceded the mistress's request, however, and most neighbours were prepared with their answer upon the messenger's arrival. The butler of every house returned the message, 'It is with my master's sincere regret he cannot place himself at your disposal!' before pulling the door tight closed. The messenger, being Jack, was in a prominent position to tell us that several of those good gentlemen 'were certainly in town' and, at the time he went calling, they were 'most surely at home!'.

Following Jack's appeal to our neighbours' goodwill, two or three were encouraged to discover what was the big to-do. Chance and Lady Fortune deigned these visitors should keep their ignorance and soon they passed on the news that there was little reason for such fuss. Then Mistress and Master Hunter, that apparently must have returned to the city in such a hurry, did come at the invitation of our mistress, and they were cordially escorted by her to every place the spirit had showed itself. Since they wished to see our hauntings, but also very much did not, it was the part of them that did not that had them leave without polite farewell when the thickset Master Hunter caught a glimpse of something not of this world hanging a foot above the stairs.

'Mistress Atkins,' he wheezed, once he had pushed his equally portly wife into the safety of their carriage and his mouth was freed to talk again. 'I do declare, that midwife lived here in this house nigh on twenty years. Believe this, for I am not mistaken. 'Tis her, I tell you.' He became more comfortable with his distance from the house. 'Bear with me in this; are you acquainted with how she did die? Was there mystery in it? I ask you to examine the case, for it is a fact most renown that such poor afflicted souls are unable to rest for reason of their needing to find revenge and retribution for their unnatural death. It is the very essence of such things, you shall see. Until the source of her torment is discovered, I am convinced you will not be rid of her.'

With this, he whipped his horse and off he went at a trot.

That very night, Eerie noises, clunks and bangs had us curling deep beneath our blankets. When I heard Faith whisper the words of the Lord's Prayer as quiet as her breath, I joined my voice to hers, our hushed voices murmuring like a breeze through dry grasses of summer, missing only the sound of the crickets. I cannot remember when we slept.

At first light of day, Faith took her packed bag, little more than a piece of cloth tied around with ends-of-threads, and returned from whence she came to her Aunt's house in Cheapside. I never did see more of her.

Into my own winter cape I wrapped my scant belongings, then followed in Faith's footsteps and informed Mrs Thomas I would not, nay, could not, stay longer in a place of such ungodliness. She informed me, on this matter, I would have to speak to the mistress about it, since her own bags were already packed and she and her husband were ready to leave as soon as he found a place for them to go to. For that reason, she said, she was in no position to speak for the mistress. And so I went to Mistress Appleton.

Mistress Appleton insisted I stay, and straight-away returned the borrowed reins of the problem of the haunting to her husband, for she was not prepared to be plagued by her entire staff leaving and begged him to quickly resolve the matter. Mr Appleton, understanding at last the gravity of the whole of it, set off in great haste to find a person who would show pity for our plight and exorcise the ghost.

First came a ruddy-faced man of the cloth that had no compunction in taking money for his gift, if gift it was. Despite his lively chants and rituals, the quacking man was not our saviour and did not rid us of the strange and unnatural happenings. Then came a younger man from a nearby parish, who splashed all over with holy water and said words of exorcism that were as ineffective as they were wet.

Last came the well-dressed pardoner with long, dirty grey hair and smelling of foreign perfume. Behind the master and mistress, all curious servants followed him from room to room, stopping when he stopped and moving forward when he did. He summoned the ghost in the dining room, the corridor, the kitchen and every place anyone had reported any strange thing. He promised to it a confession and a pardon, though the mistress's inquiries assured her the previous house-holder was not inclined towards Popery, a thing I had memory of as I shall explain in good time. The master was of the mind that, if naught else had heretofore worked, the ghost might be susceptible to the persuasion of confession in order to free its soul from our world.

No ghost or any other disgraceful apparition appeared that day, or the next. We all begun to wonder if the pardoner had not after all succeeded in banishing it where the others failed. And, with the threat of any other such happenings put aside, and Jack telling me in the strongest terms I would be a fool to leave without work to go on to, I stayed. We were all of a happier disposition now that we were free to do our tasks undisturbed.

But that was before Tuesday the 16th day of March, when events took a fearsome turn.

The night of that day was by far the worst in all my life.

Chapter Four

Mistress Atkins

'Only the best will suit, Mary,' the mistress told me. 'I have in mind this night should be a night of passion with my husband, and these sheets will not do. If they give me no comfort, I am sure Master Appleton will itch and scratch rather than take the time to find me in them!'

I nodded and bobbed briefly and left the room, for she did not expect an answer, only that I do her bidding.

The linen cupboard was in the large closet at the other end of the hallway; too far.

The candle fluttered hot against my fingers in every draught, more so when I moved too swiftly or if I forgot to shield it as I turned into the room. Each time the flame shrunk down to the base of the wick, I held my breath and trembled. I should have refused to go alone to fetch the bed clothes and would surely have done so had Faith stayed. Though, had Faith stayed, it would rather have been she who was tasked to do such things for the mistress. Again I lamented it was not I that had left and that I had been so easily swayed by the mistress's plea to stay. This night might hold the anticipation of passion for the mistress, but it filled me with deep unease and foreboding as I hurried through the corridor to carry out the errand.

But I could not begrudge the mistress and master their night together. Indeed, I should count myself most fortunate in their kindness and charity, their having made use of me as a maid this last six months after they took the house. Especially when they were under no obligation to do so. Perhaps they would not have shown me so much sympathy, had my situation not been most unfortunate and somewhat tragic. And I say unfortunate for, some weeks beforehand, my story looked to have a future so very different. The great aunt, a splendid and industrious midwife that lived here for some two decades, and with whom I was arranged to take up apprenticeship did, with great inconvenience to myself, die all too soon after my arrival. Having no other relation to whom I could turn, and my spirit cast down, I was sorry for not having come sooner to learn the craft, for it would have saved me from a life of certain servitude.

'Confound that girl!' Teeth tight-clenched and chattering, I cursed Faith's boldness in leaving with no employment awaiting her, even whilst desiring to find some of that same character in me and finding it lacking.

Once in the closet, I placed the candle upon the chest-of-drawers beside an unlit lamp. When I turned and saw it cast my shadow upon the tall oak linen-press from where I would fetch the bed clothes, I returned to the chest-of-drawers and moved the candle to some other place so I could better see what I was doing. Forsooth! It was dark this night! And cold. A draft crawled beneath my shawl and made my skin pimple.

Then my hairs stood further to attention, if that was at all possible. A blazing light from the linen press behind me caused my shadow to be cast beyond the candle, large and sharp, on the wall. The darkness in the corners of the room gone, the fiery light, as Mr Thomas had said, like the light of the summer sun, made invisible the flicker of the small flame. At first, I dared not turn and discover what unnatural and frightening blaze diminished the candlelight so, but I found I must, if only to know what danger would confront me. What should I encounter when I turned?

With difficulty, for my neck was fixed tight and could not move, I twisted my body. Then, when I saw the apparition sat atop the linen press, I forced my feet to turn and be straight with the rest of me. And, when I faced full on the thing that would confront me, I was glad of my balance, for I would surely have otherwise fallen.

'Mary.'

It knew my name.

Without a single doubt, the ghost had come for me.

And with that one word, fear, both sensible and insensible, locked me tight. My chest hurt and I could not breath. Nay, I could not have moved if that creature had assailed me right there and then. And if I could have hidden, I suspect that would not have protected me.

What gave it reason to seek me out? No worse than any other, did I not live a good life? Did I not pray in church and live with honesty? Reminded of the church, I fumbled beneath the hem of my neckline with both hands and found the thin, hard chain I did search for and pulled forth my cross.

'Begone, you Devil! Begone!' I raised the cross toward that unnatural light, high and with my arm outstretched until it ached. 'Away with you. You cannot have me!'

The only answer it did give was to repeat that one word, 'Mary'.

The word stretched long into time, not an echo but growing unwieldy inside my head and body. That it was my name made it not an urge but a command to listen. Every part of me pricked with something sharp. My skin stung as if I stood in a swarm of angry wasps. Heedless of this, I bravely challenged the greater of the two evils.

'Why do you hound me so?'

I did briefly inquire of my legs if they would run, but found they would not obey. So, I did not run or scream though all was too strange and did not make good sense to me. Truly, I expected the vision to fly at me and steal my soul before I could defend myself. It did nothing but sit there upon the press, quiet and grim. Even barely able to draw in my breath, above the waft of burning tallow candle I caught wind of something the like of burning sulphur, no doubt brought with it from whence it came.

My arm wearied of holding high the cross, but I did not let down my guard. I could not depend on it that it did not wish me harm. With difficulty, I called upon that deeper courage a man must surely find before battle. An answer I should have, for I had done nothing that justified the Devil or his minion to seek me out. However, I feared one without roots in this world would not, nay, could not, give worldly consideration to my question and would waste no time on such. Yet I must ask it.

'What will you have of me, that you alarm every person in the house to find me? You must surely have better reason than to frighten me.'

At the sound of my voice, my heart beat with such alarm I thought I might faint. Unlike the voice of the spirit, which filled my head rather than the room, my voice was loud and drew attention to me.

'Find them, Mary. Find them and bury them.' Again, I knew the repeated words could only have come from the ghost, but the sound of them came from inside.

When it did not immediately come for me, I altered my impression that it had only one intention. Such pause gave me to examine it anew. I squinted at the light and saw in it something familiar, but could not grasp any certainty in it. 'Twas a countenance I knew and should not easily forget. If I could but find the like of it in my memory, I may know its intention.

'What should I find?' It surprised me how my voice, though loud to my ears, now wavered only a little, belying how my body shook a lot. 'What must I bury?'

'Find them, Mary. Bury them. Pray for them.'

On the Holy Bible, I swear I did know that voice, though I was used to it in my ears more than in my head. I had known the owner of it for little enough time, but time enough to know something of it.

'Find them, Mary. I wronged them. More in death than life.'

It used my name. I remembered the shout of our neighbour, Master Hunter, before he raced away in his carriage.

'Mistress Atkins!' The old midwife came sharp to mind. 'Mistress Atkins. Mother Atkins. If that be you or only a semblance of you, I would know it. Show me a sign that I should know 'tis truly you and no other.' She did nothing. She said nothing. In the short time I knew her, Mistress Atkins was never short of a thing to say. Had I indeed caught the Devil out in his trickery?

Then, when I would openly revile it, it spoke again.

'Prick up your ears, girl.' The imperious voice held familiarity. 'Listen.'

In that, I let go of my cross and dropped my arm. 'Twas indeed Mistress Atkins, for she always chided me thus, even when I was attentive to every word.

'Mistress Atkins! 'Tis you, of that I am certain.' With recognition came a great deal of relief. This good woman could wish me no harm, of that I was equally certain. 'Explain yourself. I hear your plea, but understand none of it. Tell me what you want of me.'

Now the likeness of my old relation was made true, I clearly saw her character within the light and, once I saw it, she became as a solid earthly thing, even if she was not. Her more solid appearance did not, however, make her speak more plain.

'Find them, Mary. Find them beneath the stones. Bury them as they should have been buried.'

Strange that I could hear her words with greater clarity now I knew who she was.

'Stones? What stones do you speak of? What should I find there? I tire of your riddle! Speak that I might fathom it.'

When she faded back within the light I was sorry for my outburst. Now I knew it - she - had a name I was acquainted with, I would not be best pleased if my sharp tongue gave her cause to leave without revealing her secret.

After a time, she became clearer once more.

'Take up the stones...'

'What stones do you speak of? And where must I find them?' I barely suppressed my impatience, for she did repeat the same thing too often.

'Where first I came back.'

'The dining room!' There came to mind a terror-stricken Mrs Thomas, rocking her head back and forth. And the devilish shadows of the fire.

'Find what lies beneath. Lay them to rest.'

The ghost flickered like the candle flame, bigger, darker, filling the room with jumping shadows.

There were no stones I knew of in that room.

'What stones, I ask you? And for what do I search?' She still made no sense with her talk of stones and burial. Surely, she could not intend the meaning I took from her. 'Speak you of a thing or of a body?' Just as the seed of bravery had come without my calling upon it, her silence drew an answer to my question from within. 'A thing cannot find rest, only a person's soul. Then you must speak of a person. Is it for your own murdered body you would have me search?'

Six months or more ago, I once heard Mrs Atkins tell me to place the milk on the stones by the fireplace when she meant the tiles. She must mean the tiles.

Before she next spoke, it seemed she did shrink. If she yet lived, I would have thought she sighed.

'There are two.' She was not so self-assured in this and spoke quieter. I thought she spoke still of the tiles, but I was soon disowned of this false notion. Still in her lowered voice she went on. 'It shames me, what I have done.' Again, she stopped and I was fearful of what she might say. Then she grew larger, brighter, her words louder. 'Cast out by the parish,' she boomed. 'Wanted by none.' As the parish cast out the unwanted, so her hands cast out her words.

'What?' This was a thing I had not heard before. I heard nothing of the mistress cast out. She was, from all sides, a good woman and a good midwife, well-liked by all I did speak to. 'Tell me, Mistress. What did they do to you?'

"Twas desperation.'

'Tell me of it.' My every sympathy went out to her for her suffering.

'I could not help them.'

'Them? What is this 'them' you speak of?' I asked in confusion. It seemed her shame did not after all come from being cast out from the parish, but for neglect of some persons in need. Some persons cast out.

'Wretched beyond hope. They cried.' Her voice almost disappeared. I did wonder if a ghost, having none, could wring its hands, for that's what it seemed she did. 'I was merciful. Ended their pain.'

'You ended their pain? Then that is a good thing, is it not?'

She scolded me, 'Prick up your ears. Listen,' and then went on stronger as if my denial gave her strength. 'Find them. Bury them.'

I no longer misunderstood.

'I see it now! 'Tis they that are dead! Did you murder them?' Without awaiting an answer, I went on. 'What manner of monster are you!' Shaking for reason other than fear, I covered my ears no longer wishing to be the vessel for confession. 'Nay, tell me no more! I will not hear it.'

My hands could not stop her voice, which still came from within.

'Bury Them!' Her imperious voice filled my head, perhaps even the room.

'And if I do not?' I would not be part of this.

'You must,' she said.

'But if I do not?'

'I will stay.' Said with such finality I could not like. 'Until it is done.'

'Stay? You cannot! You must not. You cannot, I say!' Her words cast me in shadow. I would never be rid of her, not as long as I lived? Unthinkable!

'You must do it. Swear it.' She rose to intimidating heights, shrinking me.

I would not be threatened in that way, but thought of nothing to say. I squeezed my lips together and clenched my teeth. Then I thought again of her staying.

'You will go if I swear to do what you ask?'

'Swear it, girl. I stay 'til it's done.'

'Under the tiles you say?' I wanted no part of it. 'The master and mistress will never allow it.' If indeed this was no sham, and I felt sure my eyes and ears did not deceive me, then two bodies lay beneath the floor in the dining room. It did not seem right we should not have sensed they were there. I swallowed. Even if the

Appletons were distressed to hear of this, Mistress Appleton would never in her life allow any to touch her hearth. Not her cherished fireplace from overseas. Nevertheless, the ghost would not, or could not, go unless I did solemnly swear it.

Again, her voice came strong and clear. 'Give me your oath.'

No matter the wickedness of her deed, the two she spoke of did not deserve to lay there without proper burial. Worse, this horrid apparition had sworn to haunt me to the end of days. It was not to be borne! And so, intending to say more to her on her detestable lack of morals, I swore there and then I would do as she asked.

'I give my oath,' I said.

No sooner than I did, the room became black, darker than any natural darkness.

She was gone. The words I wished to say staying unsaid.

And in the darkness my eyes burned from the recent light.

As that miserable wretch had taken to her grave my future as a midwife, so too had she taken the prospect of my giving her a piece of my mind, how abhorrent she was to me. I stood unmoving 'til I made out the edge of the press where the murdering midwife so recently sat, wafts of acrid sulphur no longer playing with my nostrils and throat.

If it had not been that the candle had also snuffed out, I might have straight away run to find someone, for I was in great need of comfort. Yet, there was nothing here to mark the presence of the ghost and, in the silence, I started to doubt myself and wondered if I might have suffered a turn. No, I could not have done. If I had fainted, I would surely have found myself in a heap upon the floor. I checked my mind and found my memories otherwise intact and complete for the whole day. I had not fainted.

How long I stood there with the ghost and after it was gone I did not know. The candle may have burned down some time since, but the mistress had not called for me, nor had she sent another for the bedclothes I had come for. If there were no such clues, I would have thought it so much longer.

I clasped my arms around myself and shivered so much my teeth chattered. I must speak with Mrs Black, for she was as close to a mother as I could ask for, and it was the arms of a mother I was in need of. I could not think Mrs Thomas, the housekeeper, or Jack, the master's man, would allow my lifting of the tiles. And if I were to tell the master or mistress of my adventure, they would surely cast me on the streets for lying. I would walk destitute with other poor lunatics that had lost their mind. But I had given my oath and must do it.

Mrs Black would know what to do.

Chapter Five

In Accord

Mrs Black did not at all laugh at me, nor did she think me taken by madness when I told her my tale. She took me straight away into her generous arms and pulled me into her ample bosom, comforting me until I stopped trembling. When I told her how the ghost had appeared to me upon the linen press, her alarm was so great she called Mr Thomas. He came presently with Jack and Percy, the three having taken to drinking ale together of late. Mrs Black told them to hold still both tongue and cup and hear what I had to say.

Jack plumped a wool-sack on the hard wood seat and sat beside me, placing one elbow on the table and leaning in close. His eyes drew the story out of me and, though I spoke to all persons, it was as if I spoke to him alone.

When I finished speaking they stayed silent, until Jack observed, 'There is naught to do but tell the mistress.' He slapped the table making us all jump. 'We must take up the tiles and discover what truth there is in it, whether anything hides beneath.'

I nodded, but said, 'She will not do it, for she has too much pride in her prized Dutch handiwork.'

'If she will not do it,' said Mrs Black, 'we must refuse to run all errands 'til 'tis done. God bless my soul, if this ghost speaks true, two persons were horribly and wickedly murdered here.' She placed her hands on her flushed cheeks.

'Zounds! Are you all quite lost in wits?' Mr Thomas waved his hands and a piece of straw fell from his sleeve. 'You talk of this ghost as if it were a common guest. 'Tis a matter most odd, our visitor being dead, and not at all in the natural way of things.

Furthermore, this ghost is no ordinary ghost, if 'tis at all possible any ghost can be considered ordinary. She admits to murder most foul. How are we to place trust in such a one? What if she plays us false? As well, I fear you are right. The master and mistress will be altogether displeased if we dismantle the hearth.'

His wife, having softly come to stand the other side of me from her husband, did agree with him on all these points, then added her own. 'If you did see it, you would not doubt this ghost was wholly unnatural. Indeed, it seems midwives cannot be trusted at all, be they ghost or not, for are we not, even as we speak, afflicted with that Popish midwife living in Newgate for plotting against the King? And did we not further hear of that one in Paris seven years ago, that hid over sixty murdered babies in her house of office?'

'And what of the one that betrayed a man's trust, tricking him into nesting with a cuckoo?' Jack said.

'Husband,' Mrs Thomas did not stop to answer Jack. 'when you ask if any man can trust the word of a midwife, I say not, for they are too easily swayed by their treacherous nature.'

I could not agree and said so. 'Sooth,' I said. 'The Cellier woman did take up residence in the King's gaol for treason, but she is not yet condemned. Yet ones such as she bring a bad name to all of her trade, for her meddling in what is not her business. She hands all midwives a sullied reputation, though they be not of her kind nor religion.' I remembered well Mistress Atkins telling me so. She told me I must be prepared for persons that were ignorant of the craft and would disapprove of me when I would practice it. My deepest regret was I would never know this for myself. I saw the others around me were not at all sympathetic to my cause. 'That one in Paris was an unnatural monster and had the monster's death she deserved. Wouldst that I could have watched her roast for her wicked, wicked murders!'

'I would have liked to have heard if she or the cats that burned with her in the cage screamed louder!' said Mrs Black.

I found I had not finished in the defence of my lost trade. Mistress Atkins should not cast further slander upon it. 'But that one in Paris did it for the worst of reasons. We do not know if that is the case with Mistress Atkins,' I said. 'Though her actions were abhorrent, it seems we are to condemn her for her compassion and unwillingness to see them suffer.' In that, I bore witness. Had she not been ashamed and remorseful when she talked of what she had done? 'Besides, we cannot know if she spoke true unless we take up the fireplace. Tomorrow, I shall ask the mistress. She can do no worse than deny me to discover the truth of it.'

Percy, smelling of the stables and in dire need of scrub, came forth and said his piece. 'In truth, she must allow it, for who could eat at a table mere feet from the bones of some poor murdered persons!'

For the first time in the six months since the Appleton household had come to this place, I found myself accepted by it. It was as if Mistress Atkins united us as one against her. Yet, did we all question the wisdom of believing first a phantom, second a midwife, third a murderer. In that, I did disagree on the distrust of midwives, for I still yearned for that life, but in all else I found myself in full agreement with their judgment.

Chapter Six

Beneath The Fire

'I believe she was earnest in all she said, ma'am.'

Mistress Appleton called for her salts of hartshorn and leaned back in her *chaise-lounge*, fanning her face with one hand, holding her heart with the other. Sickly perspiration shone through the pale powder on her skin. I had believed she would perhaps have caught wind of the events of last night and I would need only ask her permission to search beneath the floor for her to allow it. I did not expect my news and request to cause her such affliction when it was I that had suffered the vision.

I took the mistress's hand and patted it as I had seen Mrs Black do on another occasion and, shortly, she took possession of her spirits once more. I remembered to tell her what Percy had said, how the dining table might be so close to murdered bodies. That seemed to sway her better than all else.

'Though I am certain the ghost cries false, if it does not, I most strongly refuse to eat over a murderous grave!' she declared. She surprised first me, then all others, by fast commanding the tiles should be taken up at once, adding, 'We shall lay aside the ghost's claim as sham, as I have told you it will be, and let that be an end to it all!'

The whole obligation of lifting the tiles having fallen full upon his shoulders, Mr Thomas used the curved, bone-handled knife I had sometimes seen him use to take stones from a horse's hoof and dug out the mortar around the edges of the tiles. I did ponder on the irony of that carved handle a while, a bone used to seek other bones, as he worked to find a suitable place for the small iron bar with a narrow end, hired from the blacksmith for the purpose. Most everyone in the household gathered with curiosity and excitement to see such a to-do. The mistress stood by and gave instructions, unnecessary as they were, for Mr Thomas was quite suited to his task and worked with great single-mindedness.

'Take more care, Mr Thomas. They are Delft, carried a long way from Holland,' she said. Distracted for a moment from his work, when Mr Thomas looked up at the mistress his eyes showed no curiosity. Then he frowned, for he remembered how it was of the greatest importance to her, and nodded. 'Mind the corners. The corners are fragile,' she said. 'The dull-witted oaf that first laid the tiles broke the corner of the best of them, 'the shoe-maker'.'

Mr Thomas said not a word, but was mindful to make a show of painstaking care from then on, not at all reluctant to have us watch him. It took him more than half an hour in the morning to first lift both the plain white and the blue tiles - blue-painted with a milkmaid, a blacksmith and a fisherman - while taking care not to damage the cook or the shepherd. It was but a further ten minutes to take up the board beneath them.

At this time, he seemed to baulk at intruding into that place and stepped back to allow the mistress admittance to the hole. She moved not toward it but one step away. She did not desire to investigate what lay within it any more than did Mr Thomas, so she ordered Jack to find if anything lay there beneath the floor.

Jack's usual bold face paled at the suggestion, and his lips moved to refuse her, but he did as he was bid and knelt before the hole. When he leaned forward and placed his hand inside, his eyes squeezed shut, we all breathed deep and waited for him to discover what he would. He fumbled for a while but, within a short time, he withdrew his hands and shrugged, his relief quite conspicuous.

'There be naught here, Mistress Appleton. We have been teased by Mary's ghost after all.'

All eyes found me, and I became flustered. 'Perhaps she thought it a merry jape to play upon us.' The way he looked at me, I was unclear if he meant me or the ghost.

'I swear before the eyes of the Lord God Almighty,' I said. 'She stood as true as you now stand before me, and those were her words, that I should lift these tiles and a board, and we should find the remains of the ones she murdered!' I sighed out my held breath when every other person in the room did the same, but I was soon filled by dismay in its stead, for I did not wish to be marked with the name of trickery.

I fortified myself with another deep breath. I could not leave it this way. A man never did find a misplaced thing, even if it was waved before his face. If I had imagined it all, it did seem as if it were real, and I would not believe it was nothing until I had searched in that hole myself.

Jack stepped backward as I fell to my knees where so recently he had knelt. His arms were longer than mine and I wondered what gave me cause to think I should find anything when he did not. Nevertheless, my reputation was at stake, and I would test that truth before being named false or, worse, moon-sick. Although they could not throw me into the street for lunacy, else they must do likewise for Mrs Thomas, Mr Thomas and Jack. How clever was Faith, the maid that ran from here, to have escaped this dilemma!

I stretched my arm down as Jack had done, with every bit of my mind on my fingers and their probing. At first, they found only splintered wood. A spider web caught between my finger-tips and clung there; I withdrew my hand and wiped a trail of grey dust on my green apron. Again I reached in. This time I bent my arm and fumbled beneath the outside edges of the hole left by the lifted tiles, foreboding and nerves making me sharp withdraw my hand on two or three occasions, each time bringing puffs of dust. My nose itched, then tickled and tingled, and I sneezed. I sneezed again. I wiped the tears from my eyes and Percy, the stable-boy, offered me his hand-kerchief. I barely had time to be sure it was clean before I sneezed two or three times more into it. The smell of old dust stayed in my nostrils for nigh-on two days, refusing my every effort to dissuade it from doing so, a thing I most particularly desired every time it brought to mind the events that followed.

'There!' said Mistress Appleton. 'Nothing! 'Tis as I said, all imagination. We shall close the hole and let it be a lesson learned.'

Master Appleton spoke for the first time, having stood back and watched from the door. 'All nonsense, of course. Though a fine tale to tell any that will listen.'

But I was not yet prepared to give up my reputation. When I had done with blowing my nose and dabbing my eyes, I balanced myself with one hand on the floorboards and explored a different place with my other hand. I reached my arm full length into the hole, with my cheek to the floor, giving me the most peculiar view of the shoes of so many persons: the somewhat worn leather shoes of the servants, yet high polished by Percy to meet the satisfaction of Mrs Thomas the housekeeper, beside the toes of the mistress's fine-embroidered cloth shoes, lined with sewn-in beads.

Then the tips of my fingers touched something soft and yielding that could only be cloth, and within that cloth, something hard. When reason told me it must be a bone, I squealed and sharp withdrew my hand, scraping the back of it on the edge of the exposed floorboards. Percy flinched, as did the women in the room. Mr Thomas furrowed his brow.

My breath was fast and sharp.

"Tis as she said! Something is hid there. Bones, no doubt.' My touching a murdered body somehow implicated me in the deed. I buried my hand in the pit of my arm to protect it from further befoulment. I was sorry I had made the oath and must stand by it, and I admit to being excessively relieved when Mr Thomas put his hand on my shoulder.

'Stop! If you try to take up the bones, if that's what lies down there, they might be forever lost beyond our reach between the timbers. Let us find something to go beneath them and catch them if they fall.'

'Jack, I am convinced it would make the task a deal easier if we took up the boards atop the bodies.' Mrs Black was sensible of most things, but I could not see how the boards could be taken up without moving more of the ornate painted tiles around the fireplace, a thing I could not imagine the mistress giving consent to. Indeed, she did not.

'You'll do no such thing, Jack! I have told you, those tiles are in the way of being of good Dutch design, carried here at great expense to myself. You have taken up enough, I am certain. 'Tis unlikely, with relations being as they are with that country, we shall easily replace them. You must go wheresoever you keep such a thing and find a suitable vessel to catch any bones that fall, then return at once. Upon my soul, how is it that such a morbid secret has lain so close beneath our feet every day we have been here, and we never have had the sense of it! We must unfasten the bonds of it to this place as soon as we are able and do as the ghost bids us. We shall find a suitable resting place for the forsaken souls.'

If the mistress had ever spoken so many words before, I had not been present, and she appeared to take on fresh urgency. With it, an air of assurance that brought her to her full height.

Jack ran off and I own I found his nimbleness appealing for, when he ran, his baggy clothes, that too often hid how robust he was, clung to his form. While we waited upon his return, we were silent until Percy asked me, 'What wicked thing did she do to these poor innocents?' When I told him I knew not, for I would hear none of it, he accused me, 'You are of her blood, are you not? Perhaps you were pinched together with her and knew of her deed ere now. 'Tis more a wonder that you would not know of it, if you stayed under her roof, than if you were bound to her in it. I say you composed the story of the ghost as a ruse to reveal her victims to us! What do you think of that?'

I balled my fists and also stood to my full height which, without the mistress's high soles, fell short of her by at least a hand's width, and a full two hands below the top of Percy's head. I defended myself.

'How dare you accuse me, Percy Wainwright! Ask Mr and Mrs Thomas and Jack, for they did see the ghost before I, and it turned Jack's hair white, and frightened Mrs Thomas and Mr Thomas that their hair did stand up on end. How was I the cause of that, Percy? Think you, I used the craft of magic?'

'Nay, but who is to say you did not call her spirit to frighten us, and give credence to your tale?'

'You are a silly boy, Percy. Why should I have her frighten me also? I was not at all joyful at her finding me and causing me such consternation alone in the dark. At first, I did not know her and commanded her to stop hounding me, but she would neither listen nor do as I asked. She did nothing at all at my bidding.'

Mrs Thomas remembered our company and told us to stop our quarrelling. It was unseemly before the mistress. Fire burned in my cheeks, for it was not my custom to be so negligent of sensibilities. I bobbed and begged her pardon.

Between each of the exchanges, the hole drew back my attention and my curiosity, and horror had me searching the blackness therein. The others did the same, now that Percy no longer distracted them by his picking of a quarrel with me. After the mistress had dismissed our unseemly manners, we all stood silent and every eye stayed on that darkness as if the midwife herself would rise from it with furious vigour and castigate us all for our attention having wandered from the task we were here to do.

In my mind's eye, the room filled with a burning light that took all darkness from the corners and Mistress Atkins pointed at me with a finger that was all bone and no flesh, demanding to know why we had not buried them yet. That expectation had me so fearful of her appearing so, I moved back to the door and stood with the others.

Mrs Black at once placed an arm around my shoulder and pulled me close. After a further while, I thought of the two that had died here and hung my head.

Jack returned at a rush, filled with some little excitement at the drama acted out to us that day. In his hand he carried two brooms and some twine, while under his arm looked to be one of the mistress's bedsheets.

He was treated to such melancholy when he returned that he quickly hid his eagerness and stopped beside us, bent his head and joined us in prayer to the Lord God to take these souls into His care. That he was louder than the rest of us encouraged us to speak the prayer with growing assurance. We were bound then with the bodies, or whatsoever we should find beneath the boards, but hoped the spirits of them would be taken by Our Father. They had yet to have proper burial. A thing that must soon be rectified, not only for the sake of my oath and the fear of Mistress Atkins not leaving, but for the sake of the poor souls that it appeared might lie here.

'Come, Jack. What have you found we can use for the task? Let this waiting not drag us sideways any more.'

Mistress Appleton waved her handkerchief in the air in agitation then dabbed her eyes with it.

Jack did as he was bid, employing Percy to help him. In one way or another, they purposed a suitable cradle to catch any bones that might fall as they took the mortal remains from their indecent resting place. Then they both fell to their knees, one at each side of the hole. How they both reached into that hole, I could not fathom, for there was little enough space for my own small arm let alone the muscular arms of two hard-working men. As I could not, when my hand had found the bones, neither could they see the bones nor their hands, so all was done by blind groping.

Mrs Black wrung her hands much as had Mistress Atkins had done the night before. The hands of Mrs Thomas framed her cheeks, but so unthinking of them was she that she did not know she squeezed her mouth round like an egg. I closed my own mouth, for I did not wish us all to stand with our mouths agape.

Jack and Percy seemed to be searching for something that wasn't there. Our impatience for discovery could only be filled by the talk of the two as they blindly groped beneath the floor.

'There's little enough to fetch out,' said Jack.

'Perhaps the rest has fallen between the boards? They have been here a long while, if what is left is to go by,' said Percy.

'There's nothing more, Percy. I can find nothing from this side.'

'Nor I from this.'

Then there was some puffing and huffing as they made sure they had hold of everything that was there.

'Are you ready?'

'Aye, ready.'

The two worked together to carefully bring out the hidden bodies. As they drew out the poles, a lumpy bundle of rotted fabric appeared. And then it was out and that was all of it. I don't know what I expected to see, but it was a good sight more than this small bag o' bones. So small. Almost nothing.

'Is that all?' I asked. 'Where are the bodies?'

'There is no more.'

Jack and Percy stood beside the small pile resting on the sheet. I moved closer, thinking to check again if they missed anything. Jack put his hand out to stop me.

'Nay, Mary. There's none left. I am sure.'

'Is it a cat or dog?' Percy scratched his wrinkled brow.

'Nay, Percy. None would take the trouble.'

'Who will unwrap it?' Mistress Appleton came from where she had stood behind her husband. 'Let us know what we have here.'

It fell to Jack to find the ends of the material and carefully turn it until the bones within showed themselves. It was neither cat nor a dog. Two small sculls lay in a mix of what could only be the bones of two infants. Their mouths were open, and inside one of the mouths was some more of the material. It looked as if it was packed tight in there. A small ball of a like material lay near the mouth of the other.

Mrs Thomas crossed herself with her hand.

Mrs Black had both her hands over her gaping mouth, only her big eyes showing above.

The men - Master Appleton, Mr Thomas, Jack and Percy - each and every one of them, had their faces set with clenched jaws, as if they could barely restrain their anger.

I could not move, and barely knew if I spoke or did not. The horror of it!

As the silence stretched, I heard the cries of the children, and imagined them crying every day before they died and every year since they had been placed there, but it was only now, in this silence, we at last could hear them. A tear found its way down my cheek. No person could stand before a child's grave and not be moved. For it to be the grave of two murdered children made it all the more heavy upon us. When Mrs Black's arm around my shoulder shook, I looked to her and saw she too had tears. Jack told me later that she had lost many babies.

At last, Mr Thomas broke the silence.

'That murdering witch! Murdered by the very one paid to guard them from harm.

'Aye.' I did almost forget Master Appleton was there, so little had he spoken. 'A man must have confidence in a midwife as guardian, else there be none in this world a man can trust. We must tell the magistrate, for he will wish to know of this.'

'What will we do with the bones of those poor children? Mrs Black wiped her face, leaving it still shining with her tears.

'Fetch the constable,' said Master Appleton.

In my silence, I heard the others talking, but my mind was on Mistress Atkins. These bodies were proof enough I did not imagine the ghost of the midwife, but now I saw what she had done, I had no sympathy or defence for one such as her. As Mr Thomas had said, she had been paid to keep them from harm, yet here they lay with balls of cotton packed in their mouths. And I had come here to learn from her. What manner of other things would she have taught me that I would rather she had not! Not of high respectability at all, but inhuman and barbaric.

Percy left to fetch the constable with his head raised in importance for being chosen to do so. No doubt he would stop and tell the tale to any that would listen and, since we did not know how long he might take, a chair was fetched for the mistress from the dining table. The master asked for one as well and the two sat side by side next to the body remains on the sheet by the hole in contemplation of them. The servants then waited with the master and mistress, for we were all caught in the discovery. The talk was all of the murders and how long it would take for Percy to fetch the constable.

There was a moment when the sun came from behind the clouds and I jumped, for the sharpness of the light brought to mind the night before and I thought it was Mrs Atkins come to make sure the task she had set me was done to her satisfaction. If not, she would haunt me, I feared, for the rest of my natural life. And, now that her message was proved to hold credible truth, I was certain that message could only have been revealed by one with secret knowledge of her murderous deed. I must also believe the absolute proof of a spirit world from whence Mistress Atkins had come and where she had dwelled for six months past.

Moreover, with this proof came the inevitable thought that the ghost might easily haunt me not merely for my remaining days on Earth, but forever after. This, I could not stomach. The presence of the midwife was quite enough for a half hour let alone eternity. I would lief take my chances in Hades on Lake Stygian than have her castigate me for the whole of the hereafter!

By and by, Percy came back with the constable, a wheezy middle-aged man stinking of that horrid tobacco. Percy announced that he had found him in the Red Lion at High Holborn nearby Lincoln's Inn Fields, and that he told some others that followed him home to stay at the front door. It was evident, however, that they were not to be fobbed off so easily and a few men somewhat worse for wear with the liquor jostled each other in the corridor to peer in.

The constable wiped his hands down the front of his dull brown long-coat. From the smears on his chest, it looked as if that was his habit. He demanded to know the story, then asked to see the bodies, unaware he had stood beside the bodies all along. Then, on seeing the pathetic bundle of bones, he declared he would carry them to the bone-house. In that, he was over-ruled by the raucous men outside.

'Nay, let us take them to the Red Lion,' said one.

'Aye, we will walk with you,' said another.

'You will not!' said Mrs Black. 'The infants must be buried right away.'

The constable said, by all accounts they had waited fifteen years so fifteen minutes more could not harm them. Then away they went, carrying the fragile wrappings between them.

Chapter Seven

A Second Meeting

That night, when the master and mistress had returned to their living quarters and we had returned to waiting on them, I had reason to go to the dining room and clear the dishes. Having talked on the topic all afternoon with others of the household, and curious visitors, my mind was turned off from it.

As was often the way, the candles were extinguished, the flames from the fire still high enough to clearly see what I needed to do. Heavy weariness filled me after such a crushing day and my mind was wholly on finishing my tasks and taking myself to bed. The hardest labour, even above piling the dishes together, was holding open my eyes. And in that I was struggling. But a few moments later, every bit of tiredness had gone and I was utterly vigilant, for there was the ghost of Mistress Atkins! She was not there and then she was.

My whole body stiffened and my legs showed the same reluctance to move as I was becoming used. Even so, I forced them to step back from the table toward the door. She did not look at me, but was turned from me with her head bent towards the hole by the fireplace. So sad was her stance that, for a moment I was filled with sadness for her, but only for a moment. I fast remembered what she had done.

'You! You monster! You did not tell me those you murdered were but babes. You dare come back and put me through more. Why do you return when I have done what you asked?' Once I started, as King Knut could not stop the tides, neither could I stop the anger at that most dreadful of persons, her death swaying me neither one way nor another in my judgment of her.

She turned slowly and I then saw how hollow was her face. If she had substance before, she had less of it now. When she opened her mouth, it seemed as if it gaped wider than it should, and within it a darkness more solid than anywhere else in the room. Her cavernous mouth frightened me more so than her eyes, even as deep as they had sunk above her cheek bones. Her skeletal face echoed the infant skulls.

'Bury them, Mary.'

'They have been taken from here. I cannot do more,' I said.

'You gave me your oath.'

'You broke your oath as a midwife. You killed babies.' I said. 'How did you dare call yourself midwife?' Did they, the midwives, all murder babies? Or was it only the worst of them? Though I did not want the details, I could not fathom how one promised to a life of saving mothers and their babies could do what she had done. Though I had no wish to see her again, I had a strong desire to know answers to my questions.

'You know nothing of it.'

'I know I would never have done such terrible deed.'

'I did not choose the path. I did what I must.'

'There is never reason to murder, and I will not listen further to you.'

'Hear me, Mary.' I turned away, but she went on with her voice echoing as if she talked through the wall in the next room. 'Fatherless by-blows. Wanted by none. Crying. Always crying.'

'You did say so before. But a person does not murder a child for its tears.'

'Tears of pain. Hunger. Dying slowly. I took their pain.'

'You took their life.'

'I took their pain,' she said again. 'They suffered no more. I suffered since.'

'I am glad to hear so,' I said. 'Your suffering will never be enough for what you have done.'

The fire popped and cracked and spat in the silence that followed. I thought she would leave without saying more. Some part of me filled with relief, for I wanted her to go, more than I desired answers. Then, not moving from that place, still it was as if she came close to me, her voice louder and nearby.

'Prick up your ears, Mary. Do not spurn me. Death came from overseas. All were dying. London left the city.'

'London left the city? How is that possible!' I scorned her immediately, for she made no sense.

'Fleeing Death. He found us still. Remember it, Mary.'

I did. I remembered Death. Who could forget the stench of decay piled high in the street for the dead-carts! Who could forget the suffering? None that were spared could ever wash that terrible year from their mind. I nodded. A chill drew heat from wet on my cheek.

No, I would never forget the horror of being locked in with my dead mother and father, huddled either side of my two brothers in the big bed, with only a thin shroud of sheets, failing to prevent buzzing flies laying eggs in their greying flesh. Only those sheets to stop Death's hand grabbing me.

Once famine and plague had their way, Mother's body was not much more than those of my poor brothers' so that, when I dared look upon them and see their shapes, it was as if my father lay with three children. I could not make Father's arm stay on the bed, and so it hung from beneath the sheet outside the bed, his hand curling near to the floor. More than once did I throw a shoe or piece of coal at a hungry rat eating of it. My dear family, all lost in one week, now putrid and abhorrent to me.

Neither would I ever in my life forgive the guard that refused me to bring their bodies outside. 'No death carts,' he told me. 'None to fetch them from the street.' Perhaps Lady Fortune spoke in my favour to Lord Death to spare me, but it was many years before I was glad she had done so, if ever I was.

Mistress Atkins spoke more.

'Sickness everywhere. Many fled. Mothers would not have us. We three starved... for lack of a midwife's work.'

I remembered my own hunger, closed in with my dead family with nought to eat. The growing hunger was painful. Worse yet was when the hunger stopped and I knew I should die for lack of food. I begged through the window. They shook their head and hurried on with pity in their eyes, but none aided me.

The ghost of Mistress Atkins did still speak and would not go.

'They bawled and cried. No nourishment. None for them. None for me. God wished them suffer no more.'

Here she stopped.

I wanted no detail of her deed for, having seen the ball of threads in the infant's mouth, already I too well imagined the horror of it. Such heinous crime had cost her dear. More so those poor souls! No matter the reasoning of her madness, if the Good Lord had not pardoned her sin and let her in, then neither should I.

'Take thee hither, mistress; a fiery Hell awaits you! I will hear no more of it. When I came into your house, it was for your having the highest reputation, which none did question. They told me you were the best of women-kind, but now I see you are the worst. You are but a common murderer.'

Past her, the flames were shrinking and the fire dying. Even with the light of the ghost, the room became darker, colder.

'You are no judge of me.'

'I have never murdered any single person. I have never taken the life of another. In that, I am able to bring judgment on you. I am thankful you did not teach me your horrid ways. What matters anything, when everything I would have learned would have been learned from a murderer? Would you have taught me to betray innocent children? For my part, I am glad you are dead and gone!'

The light in the room dimmed and the shadows faded. Though I could not fear the person she was, I still feared the unnatural being she had become. I saw in my mind the abomination of her ghost coming upon me. I shook. Worse, now I knew what she had done. I did not know what harm she could cause me, but not knowing was worse than knowing. She had become unexpectedly hunched and small and I feared she might pounce, and yet such pathetic creature demanded pity rather than condemnation. I tried to withhold pity for her, but failed.

Her grim words came once more. Angry.

'In the midst of death, we all were dying. Good name? Their mother cast them out. For her sake, not theirs. Their arms thin. Crying without end. Forsaken by the city. Death lay waiting. I gave him them in kindness. They suffered no more.'

Now I knew without a doubt she wrung her hands. But it was not for her to take their lives. Only God could do that.

'It was not their time,' I said.

It was if she saw into my mind.

'God lay the path for me.'

'I do not believe He ever condones murder, Mistress Atkins.'

She shrunk in on herself again. 'Neither God nor the Devil claims me. Fifteen years… Warn all midwives… beware to do as I have done…' She faded and I thought she was gone. Though I could not see her now, her voice still came from the darkness in my head, barely heard. 'Bury them, Mary. Or I'll be back. Bury them.'

Again, I was left alone. The recent unnatural presence leaving the natural seeming less so. I shivered and stared at the place she had been for a long while. Somewhere in the house a door closed. Somewhere were voices, women talking. Mrs Black and Mrs Thomas. Somewhere there were other voices. The master and mistress. They talked in their bed chamber. The noises came sharp in the silence. An owl screeched close by the window. I jumped.

Mistress Atkins twice made it clear. If I did not make sure the infants were buried, she would come back. If I did never wish to see her again, I must do as she asked. As I promised.

If I did before think I could do nothing about the bones of the infants, I knew now I must. I must speak to the master and mistress straight away and beg their compassion and aid, for where the bones had gone, it was not in my power to fetch them.

Chapter Eight

An End To It

And there it is, the story in its entirety. Or, at least, as complete as it could be until this day, when I could tell the last of it.

A little after candlelight, accompanied by every solemn servant of our household in Rotten Row, Master and Mistress Appleton took to the Cheshire Cheese off Fleet Street. With faces set and heads high, they strode through the tavern door, determined to reclaim the mortal remains of those poor children that we had found and put an end to the tavern's loud and extravagant boasts. Stories and ballads of their latest show-piece abounding were morbid temptations to beguile full-pursed custom into their drinking hole these weeks past.

Having rightly measured the notoriety of the murder and the significance of the innocent victims' bones, the Appletons took it upon themselves to pay the price of the burial; their good charity would, of course, be noted and remembered. But their charity need not extend to two of everything. The death of the babes was seen by many as a single murder, a single life, so to separate them would have been frowned upon, had it been at all possible to distinguish the bones of one from the other. The mistress had, then, chosen a small, respectable length of knitted wool, decreed by the King to be the only choice of material for a shroud, to wrap the two bodies together. And together they would be placed in a small white-painted oak casket prepared by the mortician.

The drinkers gathered around to watch the mortician respectfully wrap the bones in the wool shroud and place them into the coffin. He was particularly careful not to drop any of the bones, having earlier been castigated by the mistress for holding them with the decorum of a street oaf. The sheet he lay the bundle gently upon was the tattered cloth the small bodies had been found in, the aged material I had touched beneath the floorboards. Their discovery was still sharp and clear, the strange combination of dried skin on hard bone through cobwebs and damp cloth along with the smell of dust. As he placed the bundle down, small specks of bran blew up from around the edges of the folded material. I pursed my lips. He no doubt charged for this unnecessary custom, even knowing the desiccated bones had no need of it, having no leaking fluids to absorb.

"Tis her, the one that saw the ghost.' Even as the bones were laid, all of the tavern whispered about me, for I had as much fame as they, perhaps more, and it shames me to say I took some pride in it. An old bearded man wearing a large hat with a larger feather, and a sword by his side, asked me, 'What did she say? Was it truly Mother Atkins?'

'I can tell you it was, but can you not see I am mournful for these children? I will not say more at this time, for we are here to respect the murdered, not the murderer. Perhaps you forgot to remove your hat?'

With a 'Beg your pardon, miss,' the man, made aware of his incivility, immediately took it from his head and held it across his chest.

Divers others asked me these and other questions later as we walked, and each time I gave the same answer, 'If you are patient, you shall be rewarded with the story after the poor innocents are buried and not before.' This did not stop them quizzing others of the household about the happenings, for everyone was a-chatter about it, but it gave me time to reflect on not only the sorrow of the deaths, but also on my unwilling bond with their murderer, both alive and dead. Such pinching of us together lay stones on my heart and I wished she had not chosen to spill her story to me and not any other. A thing which tied us inextricably in shame, even if it also brought me fame and flattery. If I had been made to tell the story once, I had been made to tell it a hundred times this last fourteen-night, and I was weary of doing so again.

The door opened and the bawdy-dressed man standing there in his fine lace and blue cloak said, 'Are we for the funeral? I have an invitation.' He read it out, though the cards were common enough: *You are invited to accompany the two murdered infants of Rotten Row from The Cheshire Cheese to Saint Sepulchre Church at eight o'clock promptly.'* To the nods and murmurs of assent, he took off his hat and joined the crowd. It was my hand and Jack's that had drawn the skeletons and ghosts on the border of the card before the master took it to the printer, who then had made enough for such local taverns and coffee houses interested in taking them.

The master had said, 'The by-blows may have died in anonymity, but they will be buried in notoriety; and they may have no father to bury them, but they will have a funeral as if I am he.'

No pauper burial would do for them, and a more appropriate oak casket could not have been rented by the children's own family had they claimed them as theirs. As well as the coffin, the master paid the fee for both pall and knell, and a token feast for afterward. They would not have had such a generous funeral, I was certain, had they not become famous all over London.

The mistress draped the white pall, embroidered with an ornate cross, over the casket. Then, Mr Thomas, having been chosen to bear the paltry weight of the all-too-light child-coffin — too light for even a single child — picked it up and followed the first of the procession through the door. Two women, I did not know, lit tapers from the fire and moved between the gathered persons to light their candles in anticipation of a pleasing parade that would be enjoyed by all. So many candles reflected in the numerous square windows against the darkening night, so it seemed we were twice as many and made a pretty sight. Then we followed Mr Thomas and the coffin through the heavy oak door and into the cool spring evening.

At eight of the clock promptly, as it said on the card, we set off along Fleet Street toward the final resting place. The bell tolled three rings for each child, no rings for their ages as we did not know them. The finding of the bones, and the tale of the ghost midwife, being widely sung in ballads of late, we were followed by all manner of curious men and women, and some children hanging onto their mothers' skirts or apron strings. Indeed, Master Appleton could not have measured the fame of the events more precisely, though he was given some clues beforehand.

The discovery of the murders had cause so many tongues to wag all over the city that many of those that followed us had already come calling at Rotten Row to see where the little ones were found. Mr Appleton had given instructions that the hole by the fire should be covered by evening and night with a strong board, so no foot nor leg might fall through and be the cause of a miserable accident. By day, however, the board was removed and the hole laid bare for the curious, the horrified, the scandalized and those simply wanting to pay respects to the murdered babes. Most expressed agreement about the horror of a so-called trusty midwife displaying such terrible cruelty.

No matter that the bones were carried away by the constable and given to The Cheshire Cheese to make a show of them as they will, many still found satisfaction in seeing the hole in the floorboards. It was proof enough of the events of this story. For those that wished more evidence, they had happily waited their turn in the tavern, and stayed to drink a cup or two of ale afterward.

Those in the procession were of a more practical nature. Their desire was only to be part of a lively event, carrying candles and lighting the way between Fleet Street and the church, happy and grateful for their surviving young'uns skipping at their side. It was a pretty procession, if not wholly solemn. The deaths being a long time since, there was cheer rather than tears in the hearts of most. Even deep in reverie, the chitter-chatter slipped in: 'I heard the children rose from the dead to hound the servants of the house!' and 'Did you see the skin and hair on the bones in the box? It brought baby Samuel to mind. A sad affair and no mistake.'

It was no mistake, however, that Master Appleton chose that we should walk from Fleet Street to Saint Sepulchre along the Old Bailey road and past the court, for he was of the mind that if we could never find satisfaction in the charging and committing of Mistress Atkins for her crime, perhaps she would feel the breath of the law as we passed it by. Mistress Appleton was in accord with him on that and said the scales would tip against the midwife and she would surely feel the Sword of Justice pierce her spirit. If Mistress Atkins did feel the sword plunge into the place her heart should have been, there was no sign of it.

At the churchyard, the procession circled the dug-up ground, with those that came last filling the gaps in the crowd. The coffin was lowered by ropes into a hole that was larger than it should have been, the grave-diggers not understanding how dry and small the corpses had become over time. This was the cause of some concern as the coffin went down. It bumped first one side then another side, much as a bumble bee trying to get out. With each bump, I half-expected the bones to spill into the darkness below before words were said and was glad to see it set down safely. My duty to both dubious relation and murdered children fulfilled.

None could, or did, say it was a lavish affair, but it was simple and decent enough.

Standing behind some persons smelling strongly of Lavender, and amongst all the pretty candles flickering in the breeze, I could not help but think of another time, many years into the past. And try as I might, I could not prevent resentment marring the good deed of burying the babes. For when I saw the candle-lights and the gathering of so many with their heads bent in prayer, it brought to mind the ungallant throwing of my parents and siblings into the death cart after my entombment with them had ended. As putrid carcasses. The smell was so bad I did not stay to see the cart ride away, but went straight to the river and breathed the clearer air that blew over it. I could not join the others in closing my eyes for fear of sharpening the picture of my family's rotting corpses when they were already clear enough.

Instead I gave the whole of my attention to the tiny jumping flames behind the shielding hands of the mourners.

I discovered from the excitement and the general babble as we left the graveside, it was only for reason of association with the ghost that so many had come today, a thing I did not have a single doubt about already. If these children had been murdered yesterday, like as not there would be many fewer, if any. Something in that gave me to put away my resentment of the crowd, for these people had no better, nor more lasting, thoughts about those being buried than any ever had of my family.

Instead of jollying along with the others back to Rotten Row to eat, drink and make merry, I told Mrs Black I would rather stay awhile longer and would follow soon after. Though surprised, and with a deal of concern, she bustled ahead of the crowd to be sure of being home first to serve the modest feast. Alone in the near-dark, I returned to the graveside. I said my own silent prayer that no more wicked deeds had been done by Mistress Atkins and there should be no more visitations from her ghost. I sighed and took a handful of loose dirt that had been dug from the hole, throwing it upon the lid of the box. It made a quiet patter like rain. The small bodies had been laid to rest, and that should be an end to it. I thought again how Mistress Atkins might have put an end to two crying children, and again I was grateful she had not informed me of the details.

I was alone in the graveyard. I should have been fearful, but the fear stayed away. Strange it did not come. With such frightening things I had seen, I could not bring myself to be scared of the dead, only the living. But, then, there were plenty enough of the living that might come by that I should have reason to be afraid of. If I had taken the trade of midwife, I thought, I would have attended births at night and regularly faced such persons that wandered the streets after dark. Saving children such as those that lay in the casket below would have been my life.

I took another handful of dirt and simply held it. The cold earth took the warmth from my palm. Silently and inside, I cried for my mother. I cried for my father and brothers. And when I was done my private crying, in their name I threw another handful of dirt on the lid with the first and set off for home. My thoughts more on what I might have become had Mistress Atkins trained me, I said 'Good evening' to the graveyard guard at the gate as I left. He raised his hat in reply. Perhaps I would find another midwife to take me as apprentice, and I could make amends for the wrongs of my old teacher. More so than ever, I desired to devote my own life to the saving of others, to give them a chance where there was none. Young lives such as these we'd buried today.

'You going my way?' A figure stepped away from the stone gatepost in front of me. I covered my mouth so as not to scream. It was only Jack. He was not wearing his usual loose clothes, but his rather fetching church clothes.

'That very much depends, Jack. Are you heading to the burial feast?'

'Where else, I ask you!'

'Why then are you here and not there?' I asked, hoping for an answer that would please me. I was not disappointed.

'How ungallant would I be not to wait on the most famous maid in London?' He offered me his arm. Without a second thought, I put aside ghosts and murders and what might have been and slipped my arm in his. Immediately, he pulled his elbow to his side to bring me closer, and in this very agreeable manner we made our way slowly back to Rotten Row.

The End

References

Clark, Sandra, Women and Crime in the Street Literature of
    Early Modern England, Palgrave Macmillan (24th Oct
    2003)
Evenden, Doreen, The Midwives of Seventeenth Century
    London, Cambridge Studies in the History of Medicine
    (1st Nov 2006)
Kelly, Deidra, Death, Dying and Funerals in the Seventeenth
    Century, Funerals in the Seventeenth Century 6th Nov
    2012
Laqueur, Thomas, Bodies, Death, and Pauper Funerals,
    Representations, No. 1 (pp. 109-131 (Feb. 1983)
Lowndes, William Thomas, The Bibliographer's Manual of
    English Literature, Volume 2, pg 1311q1ws, William
    Pickering, London (1834)
Pepys, Samuel, [searches:] "dogs, tongs and shovels" (7th Sept
    1663), andiron (16th Sept 1664), The Diary of Samuel
    Pepys (1663/1664)
Whittle, Jane and Griffiths, Elizabeth, Consumption and Gender
    in the Early Seventeenth-Century Household: The World
    of Alice Le Strange, Oxford University Press (2012)
Woods, Robert, Children Remembered: Responses to Untimely
    Death in the Past, Liverpool University Press (2006)
(unknown author), A New Ballard of The Midwives Ghost, (1680)
    English Broadside Ballard Archive (Ebba.english.ucsb.
    edu EBBA ID: 20763), University of California, Santa
    Barbara

Online

Bell, Peter, *A Short History of Stretchers*, (30th April 2010) http://www.ambulanceservices.co.uk/NAPAS%20Training%20Files/Training%20Files/Short%20History%20of%20Stretchers.pdf

Cann, Helen, *The Coffee House Tour: Mapping London & 17th century coffee house culture*, Fine Art, http://www.helencannfineart.co.uk/the-coffeehouse-tour

Davison, Anita, *Seventeenth Century Funeral Practice*, Hoydens and Firebrands, (23rd Jul 09) http://hoydensandfirebrands.blogspot.com/2009/07/17th-century-funeral-practices.html

Elaine, *The Midwives Ghost*, The Early Modern World (20th Mar 2011) http://earlymodernwomen.blogspot.com/2011/03/ballad-of-midwife-ghost.html

Emsley, Clive, Hitchcock, Tim and Shoemaker, Robert, *Crime and Justice - Policing in London*, Old Bailey Proceedings Online (25 March 2018) www.oldbaileyonline.org, version 7.0

Maitland, William, *"The history and survey of London : from its foundation to the present time"* [NOTE: Scroop Court where Rotten Row actually was situated, opposite St Andrews Church] Internet Archive (1732) Boston Public Library https://archive.org/stream/historysurveyofl02mait/historysurveyofl02mait_djvu.txt

Martin, Randall, *Women, Murder, and Equity in Early Modern England* (Limited preview) (12th Dec 2007) Routledge https://books.google.co.uk/books?id=TbGTAgAAQBAJ

Mieszkowski, Katharine, *The filthy, stinking truth*, Salon (30th Nov 2007) https://www.salon.com/2007/11/30/dirt_on_clean/

Orr, Brian J., *Seventeenth Century Burial*, The Reformation, http://www.thereformation.info/seventeenth_century_burials.htm

Russan, Lilian and Ashmore, *Full text of "Historic streets of London : an alphabetical handbook"* [NOTE: UNION COURT. Holborn. (E.C.2.) : Originally called Scroop's Court], Internet Archive, (1923) https://archive.org/stream/historicstreetso00russuoft/historicstreetso00russuoft_djvu.txt

Stow, John, Kingsford, C.L. (Editor), *A Survey of London: Reprinted from the text of 1603, with introduction and notes, volume 2*, Cambridge University Text (2015) https://books.google.co.uk/books?id=WlwQCAAAQB AJ&dq=Stow,+John,+Kingsford,+C.L.+(Editor)+A+Sur vey+of+London:+Reprinted+from+the+text+of+1603,+ with+introduction+and+notes,+volume+2&source=gbs_navlinks_s

Ukers, William H. (editor), *Map showing the location of many of the old London coffee houses previous to the fire of 1666*, All About Coffee, The Tea and Coffee Trade Journal Company (1922) New York, http://archive.org/stream/all aboutcoffee00ukeruoft#page/76/mode/1up

Yetter, Elizabeth, *10 Horrors Of The Great Plague Of London*, (February 15, 2017) http://forums.canadiancontent.net/history/150194-ten-horrors-great-plague-london.html

Zuvich, Andrea, *The (Not-So-Hygenic)Personal Hygene of the 17th Century*, The Seventeenth Century Lady   (22nd Jan 2013) http://www.andreazuvich.com/history/the-hygiene-of-the-17th-century/

Seventeenth Century Law and Order, Hertfordshire Mercury (15th May 1931) http://www.hertspastpolicing.org.uk/content/crimes_and_incidents/policing_before_the_police_force/seventeenth-century-law-order

Rotten Row [NOTE: not the Rotten Row where story takes place] London Remembers https://www.londonremembers.com/subjects/rotten-row

Lye and Chamber Lye: Ashes, lye-making, black soap, urine, Old and Interesting (20th Jun 2007) http://www. oldandinteresting.com/washing-with-lye.aspx

Andirons, Wikipedia,   https://en.wikipedia.org/wiki/Andiron

Fire Dogs, firebacks, Wikipedia, https://en.wikipedia.org/wiki/ Fireplace_fireback

British Police History, City of London Police, (Last updated 18 November 2013) https://www.cityoflondon.police.uk/ about-us/history/Pages/British-Police-history.aspx

Life in the Living Room, The Geffrye Museum of the Home https://www.geffrye-museum.org.uk/collections/ thematics/17th/

Our History, The Tallow Chandlers Company, https://www. tallowchandlers.org/about-us/the-company/our-history

The History of Soap, The Soap Kitchen https://www. thesoapkitchen.co.uk/acatalog/The-History-of-Soap.html

Cooling out a Hot Horse, Equisearch For People Who Love Horses (July 1st 2005) https://www.equisearch.com/articles/ cooling-out-hot-horse-17252

Images

"Chantier de Cathedrale, Bible de Maciejowski.gif" [image], (proof of litter in 17th century) http://medieval.mrugala. net/Enluminures/Divers/Chantier de Cathedrale, Bible de Maciejowski.gif

"Maître du Couronnement de Charles VI" [image], (proof of medieval stretchers) https://en.wikipedia.org/wiki/ Stretcher#/media/File:BNF_Fran%C3%A7ais_9749,_ fo._67v,_c.1380.jpg

"Plague Pit" [image], (proof of litters used in 17th century) http://i1.wp.com/listverse.com/wp-content/ uploads/2017/02/Plague-Pit.jpg?w=632

Author Notes about
The Ghost Midwife

This story is based on the broadsheet *A New Ballad of The Midwives Ghost*, printed in London in 1680, a ballad I discovered whilst researching Elizabeth Cellier (a bold Catholic midwife caught up in the Popish Plot) for my award-winning novel *The Popish Midwife*. Many ballads of the time were the equivalent of news stories made more enjoyable and memorable by putting them to music. The songs might have been sung in taverns or coffee houses, or learned and sung in the home or elsewhere.

Although I found little more information about the events of this story than was present in the verses, it caught my imagination, being a record of the day about what one midwife did with illegitimate children placed in her care. I wonder how representative this behaviour was of the day and of the trade, considering two other stories of the time.

Thirteen years later, in 1693, another midwife, Mary Compton of Poplar, London, was found guilty of the murdering of six children. The 'by-blows' (illegitimate charges) in her care were starving and neglected. One of these children raised the alarm whilst the midwife was out and, when those going to their aid entered her house, they found dead bodies in the cellar. As is likely with Mistress Atkins, these children were placed by the parish into the midwife's care, she being paid to look after them.

Far worse was the trial and conviction in Paris of a midwife for unimaginable crimes seven years before this story took place, mentioned here in the story for its notoriety. In 1673, a midwife was tried and convicted for the murder of at least 62 children found in her 'house of office' (her privy, or outside toilet). Her fate was gruesome; she was placed in an iron cage and hung over a fire to roast to death, with a number of live cats locked in the cage with her in the same way that cats were sewn into the effigy of the Pope for burning in London's annual anti-Catholic processions.

There has been suggestion that perhaps some of these bodies might have been babies the midwife didn't know what else to do with. It's impossible to know how they disposed of such bodies in a city, particularly when infant mortality was so high. What nobody stopped to ask her was, did she kill the babies, or was that where she disposed of stillborn babies for their mothers?

Conversely, there was evidence against Mistress Atkins and Mistress Compton (if you consider the testimony of a ghost as evidence). The proof against the midwife in Paris was purely on the bodies. Today that might be considered indisputable evidence, and it was certainly taken as such then, but did anyone ever stop to ask how so many bodies came to be there? I would love to know!

Certainly, different times called for different practices. For instance, surgeons back then were often grave-robbers. Of course, grave-robbing was a crime then as now, but then it was seen by the surgeons and doctors as a necessity so that they could save lives. That was often the only way they could practice their cutting and sewing skills before using them on the living.

I know many readers of historical fiction enjoy knowing the stories they read are based in fact; learning a little history while being entertained. In that spirit, I've included below a copy of the broadsheet with a transcription, so you can see which parts were straight out of the ballad and which parts were imagined to hold the story together. After that, I've added an article of why I love seventeenth century midwives. They had a mixed reputation, but one thing I love about them is that they left their mark.

A New BALLAD *of*

The Midwives Ghost:

Who appeared to several People in the House where she formerly lived in *Rotten-Row* in *Holbourn, London,* who were all afraid to speak unto her, but she grow-ing very *Impetuous,* on the 16th. of this Iustant *March,* 1680, declarred her mind to the Maid of the said House, who with an Unanimous Spirit adhered to her, and afterwards told it to her Mistris, how that if they took up two Tiles by the Fire-side, they should find the Bones of Bastard-Children that the said Midwife had 15 years ago Murthered, and that she desired that her Kinswoman *Mary* should see them decently Buried; which accordingly they did, and found it as the Maid had said. The Bones are to be seen at the *Cheshire-Cheese* in the said place at this very time, for the satisfaction of those that believes not this Relation.

To the Tune of, *When Troy Town,* &c.

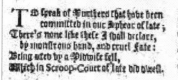

To speak of Murthers that have been
   committed in our Sphear of late;
There's none like these I shall declare,
   by monstrous hand, and cruel Fate:
Being acted by a Midwife fell,
Which in Scroop-Court of late did dwell.

Mistris Atkins she there was call'd,
   of reputation good alway;
Till Death did send his piercing Dart,
   and told her that he could not stay:
But she must to the Stigion Lake,
For murthering Babes for Parents sake.

She seeing now her time was come,
  most bitterly began to weep;
And lifting up her hands on high,
  she took a shape, not lasting deep:
Six months ago, as I am told,
Before she did this some unfold.

Therefore not to detain you long
  to this discourse, I now will press;
Which is a truth assuredly,
  as many know, and you may guess:
'tis plainly told herein,
Whereas their bones are to be seen.

The House where now this Widow liv'd,
  hath very much disturbed been;
With Apparitions very strange,
  the like whereof hath not been seen:
Sometimes resembling of her shape,
At other times Hells mouth to gape.

Which put the people in great fear,
  that there had taken up abode,
Being loath for to disclose the same,
  for fear expersions they should load
On her whom they really thought
Could never be to Lewdness brought.

But still they daily was oppress,
  with dismal shapes, and Rattlings strange
That by no means they could not rest,
  being very loath from thence to range:
They told some Neighbours secretly,
Wishing them their faith to try.

To speak unto this Spirit strange,
  if that occasion they saw;
But they thereby was daunted quite,
  and very much was kept in awe:
The hair o'their heads standing on end,
To see their late Familiar Friend.

She finding none that would reply,
  importunate at last did grow;
Th' 16th. of this Instant March,
  unto the Maid reveal'd her Woe:
Who then was by her Mistris sent,
To fetch Night-cloaths Incontinent.

pray Virgin stay, then quoth the spirit,
  for I to you will do no harm;
And tell Mary whom I love most,
  that I hereby, her now do charm;
Two Tiles by th' fire up to take,
A Board also, and then to make

A Burial of what she finds,
  in decent and most handsome sort;
And let the World to know my Crime,
  and that I am most sorry for't:
Desiring Midwives to take heed,
How they dispose their Bastard-breed.

She having now reveal'd her mind,
  did vanish in a Flash away,
And none doth know where she's confin'd,
  until the General judgement-day:
When as she shall the answere make,
For what she then did undertake.

The Maid at first astonish'd was,
  at this which she her self did hear;
And to her Mistris did impart,
  the same that now I do declare:
Concerning of the Furthers strange,
And did not seem at all to change.

Which being throughly searched out,
  accordingly it did appear;
The Maid she spoke to is suppos'd,
  to be her kind Kinswoman neer:
That will fulfill her will, 'tis said,
She being a Religious Maid.

Good People they are apt of late,
  to condemn (most) strange things as Lyes,
To'th Cheshire-Cheese you may repair,
  for this they will you satisfie:
Having the Childrens Bones to show,
In Holborn if you to it know.

        F I N I S.

London, Printed for T. Vere, at the Sign of
the Angel in Guiltspur-Street, 1680.

A New Ballad of The Midwives Ghost

TO speak of Murthers that have been
committed in our Sphear of late;
There's none like these I shall declare,
by monstrous hand, and cruel Fate:
Being acted by a Midwife fell,
Which in Scroop-Court of late did dwell.

Mistris Atkins she there was call'd,
of Reputation good alway;
Till Death did send his piercing Dart,
and told her that he could not stay:
But she must to the Stigion Lake,
For murthering Babes for Parents sake.

She seeing now her time was come,
most bitterly began to weep;
And lifting up her hands on high,
she took a short, not lasting sleep:
Six months ago, as I am told,
Before she did this same unfold.

Therefore not to detain you long
to this discourse, I now will press;
Which is a truth assuredly,
as many know, and you may guess:
When as 'tis plainly told herein,
Whereas their bones are to be seen.

The House whereas this Midwife liv'd,
hath very much disturbed been;
With Apparitions very strange,
the like whereof hath not been seen:
Sometimes resembling of her shape,
At other times Hells mouth to gape.

Which put the people in great fear,
that there had taken up abode,
Being loath for to disclose the same,

for fear expersions they should load
On her whom they really thought
Could never be to Lewdness brought.

But still they daily was opprest,
with dismal shapes, and Lightings strange
That by no means they could not rest,
being very loath from thence to range:
They told some Neighbours secretly,
Desiring them their Faith to try.

To speak unto this Spirit strange,
if that occasion they saw;
But they thereby was daunted quite,
and very much was kept in awe:
The hair o'their heads standing on end,
To see their late Familiar Friend.

She finding none that would Reply,
importune at last did grow;
A'th 16th . of this Instant March ,
unto the Maid reveal'd her Woe:
Who then was by her Mistris sent,
To fetch Night-cloaths Incontinent.

pray Virgin stay, then quoth the ghost,
for I to you will do no harm;
And tell Mary whom I love most,
that I hereby, her now do charm,
Two Tiles by 'th fire up to take,
A Board also, and then to make

A Burial of what she finds,
in decent and most handsome sort;
And let the World to know my Crime,
and that I am most sorry for't:
Desiring Midwives to take heed,
How they dispose their Bastard-breed.

She having now reveal'd her mind,
did vanish in a Flash away,
And none doth know where she's confin'd,
until the General judgement-day:
When as she shall the answer make,
For what she then did undertake.

The Maid at first astonish'd was,
at this which she her self did hear;
And to her Mistris did impart,
the same that now I do declare:
Concerning of the Murthers strange,
And did not seem at all to change.

Which being throughly searched out,
accordingly it did appear;
The Maid she spoke of is suppos'd,
to be her kind Kinswoman neer:
That will fulfill her will, 'tis said,
She being a Religious Maid.

Most People they are apt of late,
to condemn (most) strange things as lyes,
To 'th Cheshire-Cheese you may repair,
for this they will you satisfice:
Having the Childrens Bones to show,
In Holbourn if you do it know.

FINIS.

London, Printed for T. Vere, at the Sign of
the Angel in Guiltspur-Street. 1680.

Why I Love
Seventeenth Century Midwives

If there's any group of women anywhere I have the greatest respect for, it's the midwives. The job they do, even now, requires many different roles. They support a pregnant woman before birth; they might be present at the birth and then they often provide post-birth advice and care. This means they are frequently the source of the most constant contact between the mother, her children and the medical profession throughout large portions of her childbearing years. Having a good midwife can make the difference between being comfortable and happy with the new role of motherhood, help recovering physically, and mentally and emotionally adapting to a life with a new dependent. A good midwife can help make that transition smooth; a more disengaged one can leave a new mother feeling uncertain, insecure, unhappy.

And that's now.

Three hundred years ago, almost any women could act as a midwife for the birth of a family member, friend or neighbour. And, indeed, it often fell on ladies of quality to tend to births not only one of their own household, but also of those working for them. For many of these women, the only experience they might have is of being present at other births, perhaps watching their mother or another female relative at the bedside. There was no formal training, only networking. Any woman might fall into this group.

But there was another group: midwives who regularly attended births both near and far away, and were paid for it, made a living from it. A decent living at that, in many cases. Good midwives were highly sought after, and when a woman found one, they retained them for future births and spread the word this was a midwife you could trust. These women often learned their trade through apprenticeships lasting many years, and obtained a license to practice based on the testimonials of several different women who had been birthed by them.

I've discovered something special about this group of women. They have certain qualities that make them stand out at a time when women were supposed to be subservient. Perhaps it is because they were able to retain a certain level of independence, or perhaps it is because they were given certain privileges of entry into places other women were forbidden (if the wife of a coffee house owner was having a baby, the midwife was bound to be allowed entry, when they wouldn't otherwise be). Or perhaps it is because they had to bravely walk to and from births whether by day or through dark, unlit streets at all hours of the night. Something made this group of women brave.

As I did my seventeenth century research for *The Popish Midwife*, delving into the life of Elizabeth Cellier who stood up in court for her belief, I came across Anne Hutchinson in Boston, famous for defending the right of a person to think for herself. At least three others wrote a book (Louise Bourgeois in France; and Jane Sharp and Elizabeth Cellier in England). There were many more outstanding midwives.

Another story I'm currently writing - *The French Midwife* - is different from these. It's about infamous rather than famous midwife, Marie Desormeaux. She murdered her husband and planted bits of his body to be found all over London. However, I argue that, after years of abuse, she was desperate enough to take her life into her own hands. I no way condone murder, but in that time beating your wife *was* condoned, desirable even, to bring her under control. And when that power fell into the hands of a man who physically, emotionally and sexually abused his wife, several times to the point of near-death, I can understand her desperation. It was either him or her.

Even in this awful situation, Marie showed aspects of character similar to the other midwives of the time – that inner strength, confidence and belief in herself.

So many midwives of seventeenth century stood out, whether for good or for bad; accused of witchcraft but more likely employed to search for witch-marks; of being a whore, yet conversely of their wisdom in the lore of nature and birth; of being drunks or for their calm in dealing with births going wrong. Whatever their reputation, there was something about them that brought forth strong feelings one way or another. And for that I'm grateful. It means they were talked about, recorded, for good or ill, leaving traces and trails to follow today.

If it wasn't for so many recorded incidents, ballads, court records and letters, I would never have found out so much about Elizabeth Cellier's story after I discovered her by accident (I won pages recording her trial in an auction). Once I saw what an interesting person she was, her notoriety, that she was talked about, made fun of, I was able to find clues about her in so many different places, all waiting for me to put together and create her story. I think you'll agree her story is exciting and worth reading.

In the same way, each of the midwives I write about were recorded for some outstanding behaviour or event and, because of this, we can learn something about this wonderful group of people in the past.

About the Author

Annelisa Christensen - bringing history to life.

One day, several years ago, Annelisa bought some pages of a trial, merely to hold a piece of a 300-year-old book. That purchase changed her life. The defendant in the trial captivated her and her story demanded to be told. Annelisa's debut novel, *The Popish Midwife*, is based closely on the true story of Elizabeth Cellier, an extraordinary 17th century midwife.

Annelisa's research revealed Elizabeth to be known in three areas of interest - for being a woman writer when it was much frowned upon, for being caught in The Popish Plot, and as a forward-thinking midwife - but her story was all in pieces and scattered. It was such an fantastic tale, Annelisa wanted to link it all together and share it with people of today. If Cellier could be all she was in a time of such prejudice and suppression, echos of our own time, how much more amazing would she be now when we have so much more freedom?

The Popish Midwife won the bronze award in the Christian Historical Fiction category of the Readers' Favorite international book awards 2017.

Annelisa also writes poetry and story rhymes, and is currently writing *The Midnight Midwife* (novella) and *The French Midwife* (the second full-length novel) in The Seventeenth Century Midwives series of stand-alone tales, as well as a magical realism series (University of Lights).

***

Please support the Author

Annelisa would be delighted to hear what you thought of *The Ghost Midwife*. Please, also, tell others about it and leave a review at any book place you hang out. Annelisa can be found (among other places) online:

- On Twitter: @Alpha_Annelisa
- At her website: annelisachristensen.com
- At her blog, *Script Alchemy*: www.scriptalchemy.com
- On her Script Alchemy Facebook page: facebook.com/scriptalchemy
- Goodreads: www.goodreads.com/author/show/15489090.Annelisa_Christensen
- Readers' Favorite: readersfavorite.com/book-review/the-popish-midwife
- Historical Novel Society: historicalnovelsociety.org/directory/annelisa-christensen/

With Thanks

Thank you to Tim Savage for his encouragement, for the cover and generous feedback. Thanks to my sons Joe and Connor, my daughter Carmen and my sisters Karen and Helen for their ongoing support. Special thanks to my daughter, Rhianna, for unwavering daily support. She has to put up with a lot!

Also, thanks to all the readers who read *The Ghost Midwife* and made suggestions.

Other Titles by this Author

POETRY

A-Z (SERIES)

MONSTERS (NOT) FOR BED (2017): Likened to the style of Roahl Dahl and other well loved authors, these mythical and contemporary monsters will have you chuckling out loud. (two editions: Ebook and Colour (fixed format))

***THE AUTHOR THANKS YOU FOR TAKING THE TIME TO LEAVE FEEDBACK AND LETTING OTHERS KNOW WHAT YOU THINK OF THIS BOOK. ***

Other readers depend on your feedback to help them decide whether or not this book is something they might enjoy.

The author appreciates your taking the time to leave a review because it helps to get their hard work noticed by other readers.

52461853R00056

Made in the USA
Lexington, KY
14 September 2019